An Outline of English Speech-craft

William Barnes

Copyright © 2017 Okitoks Press

All rights reserved.

ISBN: 1982074132

ISBN-13: 978-1982074135

Table of Contents

FORE-SAY..3
SPEECH-CRAFT..4
    THINGS AND THING-NAMES...7
    SUCHNESS OR QUALITIES, ...14
    TIME-TAKING. 15
    -ING Root-words (strong). 18
    Under-Sundrinesses of Time-takings. 31
    Fitting of the Time-word to all the cases of Person, Time, and Mood. 31
    Things and Time-takings. 32
    THOUGHT-WORDING, SPEECH-WORDING, ...36
WORDS OF SPEECH-CRAFT, AND OTHERS, ENGLISHED. WITH SOME
NOTES..45
    The Power of the Word-endings. 64
    The Goodness of a Speech...66
    Footnotes 69

FORE-SAY.

This little book was not written to win prize or praise; but it is put forth as one small trial, weak though it may be, towards the upholding of our own strong old Anglo-Saxon speech, and the ready teaching of it to purely English minds by their own tongue.

Speech was shapen of the breath-sounds of speakers, for the ears of hearers, and not from speech-tokens (letters) in books, for men's eyes, though it is a great happiness that the words of man can be long holden and given over to the sight; and therefore I have shapen my teaching as that of a speech of breath-sounded words, and not of lettered ones; and though I have, of course, given my thoughts in a book, for those whom my voice cannot reach, I believe that the teaching matter of it may all be put forth to a learner's mind, and readily understood by him, without book or letters. So, for consonants and vowels, as letters, I put breath-pennings and free-breathings, and these names would be good for any speech, of the lettering of which a learner might know nothing. On the grounds here given, I have not begun with *orthography*, the writing or spelling of our speech, or of any other, while as yet the teaching or learning of the speech itself is unbegun.

I have tried to teach English by English, and so have given English words for most of the lore-words (scientific terms), as I believe they would be more readily and more clearly understood, and, since we can better keep in mind what we do than what we do not understand, they would be better remembered. There is, in the learning of that charmingly simple and yet clear speech, pure Persian, now much mingled with Arabic, a saddening check; for no sooner does a learner come to the time-words than he is told that he should learn, what is then put before him, an outline of Arabic Grammar. And there are tokens that, ere long, the English youth will want an outline of the Greek and Latin tongues ere he can well understand his own speech.

The word *grammar* itself seems a misused word, for *grapho* is to write, and *graphma*, worn into *gramma*, means a writing, and the word *grammatikē* meant, with the Greeks, booklore or literature in the main, and not speech-teaching alone.

Whether my lore-words are well-chosen is a question for the reader's mind. I have, for better or worse, treated the time-words, and nearly all the parts of speech, in a new way. I have clustered up the time-words as weak or strong on their endings, rather than on their headings, which had nothing to do with their forshapening or conjugation. Case I have taken as in the thing, and not in the name of it, as case is the case into which a thing falls with a time-taking, and case-words (prepositions) and case-endings are the tokens of their cases. The word *preposition* means a foreputting, or word put before; but then *from* and *to*, in *herefrom*, and *therefrom*, and *hitherto*, and *thereto*, are postpositions.

I have tried, as I have given some so-thought truths of English speech, to give the causes of them, and hope that the little book may afford a few glimpses of new insight into our fine old Anglo-Saxon tongue.

To any friend who has ever asked me whether I do not know some other tongues beside English, my answer has been 'No; I do not know English itself.' How many men do? And how should I know all of the older English, and the mighty wealth of English words which the English Dialect Society have begun to bring forth; words that are not all of them other shapes of our words of book-English, or words of their very meanings, but words of meanings which dictionaries of book-English should, but cannot give, and words which should be taken in hundreds (by careful choice) into our Queen's English? If a man would walk with me through our village, I could show him many things of which we want to speak every day, and for which we have words of which Johnson knew nothing.

Some have spoken of cultivated languages as differing from uncultivated ones, and of the reducing of a speech to a grammatical form.

What is the meaning of 'cultivate' as a time word about a speech? The Latin dictionary does not help us to its meaning, and it might be that of the French *cultiver*, from which we should have, by the wonted changes, to *cultive*. The Romans said *colere deum* and *colere agrum*, but not *agrum cultivare*; and we may believe that *colo*, with *deus* or *ager*, bore the same meaning, 'to keep or hold (with good care),' and a speech is cultivated by the speaking as well as by the writing of it, and a speech which is sounding over a whole folkland every moment of the day cannot be uncultivated. 'Not with good care,' it may be said. Yes; most people speak as well as they can, as they write as well as they can, from the utterer of a fine rede-speech (oration), and the clergyman who gives unwritten sermons, down to the lowly maiden who dresses as finely as she can; and to try to dress herself well is a token that she will try to express herself well.

King Finow, of the Tonga Islands, gave a fine speech, as Mr. Mariner tells us, at his coming to the throne; and it may be well said that he made it, as he had made it in thought, ere he came to the meeting.

What is meant by the reducing of a speech to a grammatical form, or to grammar, is not very clear. If a man would write a grammar of a speech, of which there is yet none, what could he do but show it forth as it is in the shape which its best speakers over the land hold to be its best? To hold that a tongue had no shape, or a bad one, ere a grammar of it was written, seems much like saying that a man had no face, or a bad one, till his likeness was taken.

SPEECH-CRAFT.

Speech-craft (Grammar), called by our Saxon fore-fathers *Staef-craeft* or *Letter-craft*, is the knowledge or skill of a speech.

The science of speech in the main, as offmarked from any one speech (Philology), may be called *Speech-lore*.

Speech is the speaking or bewording of thoughts, and is of sundry kinds of words.

Speech is of breath-sounds with sundry breathings, hard or mild, and breath-pennings, which become words.

(1) A freely open breathing through the throat, unpent by tongue or lips, as in the sounds **A, E, O, OO**, which are pure voicing. The main ones in English are—

- 1. **ee**, in *meet*.
- 2. **e**, in Dorset speech.
- 3. **a**, in *mate*.
- 4. **ea**, in *earth*.
- 5. **a**, in *father*.
- 6. **aw**, in *awe*.
- 7. **o**, in *bone*.
- 8. **oo**, in *fool*.

Besides this open speech-breathing there are two kinds of breath-penning.

(2) The dead breath-penning, as in the sounds **AK, AP, AT, AG, AB, AD**, which end with a dead penning of the sounding breath.

In **AK** and **AG** it is pent in the throat.

In **AP** and **AB** with the lips.

In **AT** and **AD** on the roof.

K, P, T are hard pennings; **G, B, D** are mild pennings, the breathing being harder in the former and softer in the latter.

Then there are half-pennings of the sounding breath, which is more or less but not wholly pent, but allowed to flow on as through the nose in

- AMH,
- ANH,
- AM,
- AN,
- ANG;

as in the half-pent sounds—

AKH,

AF,	AV,
ATH,	ATHE,
ALL (Welsh),	AL,
ARH,	AR,

5

AS,   AZ,

ASH,   AJ
              (French),

half-pent by the tongue and mouth-roof.
For a hard breathing the mark is **H**, as *and, hand; art, hart.*

1 Dead Pennings, Hard	2 Half-Pennings, Hard	3 Dead Pennings, Mild	4 Half-Pennings, Mild
(1) **C**, **K**(Throat)	(5) **KH** German and Welsh	(14) **G**	(18) **GH**
(2) **NK** in *ink*	(6) **F**	(15) **NGH** like **NG** in *finger*, not *singer*	(19) **NG**
(3) **P** (Lip)	(7) **MH**	(16) **B**	(20) **V**, **BH** Irish
(4) **T**	(8) **TH** in *thin*	(17) **D**	(21) **M**
	(9) **LL** Welsh		(22) **TH** in *thee*
	(10) **RH** Welsh		(23) **L** Welsh
	(11) **S**		(24) **R** Welsh
	(12) **SH**		(25) **Z**
	(13) **NH**		(26) **J** French
			(27) **N**

Words are of breath-sounds, and some words are one-sounded, as *man*; and others are tway-sounded, as *manly*; and others many-sounded, as *unmanliness.*

There is word-strain and speech-strain.

The high word-strain (accent) is the rising or strengthening of the voice on one sound of a word, as *man'ly.*

The high speech-strain (emphasis) is the rising or strengthening of the voice on a word of a thought-wording.

The voice may both rise and fall on the same sounds, as *nō*.

In English and its Teutonic sister speeches the strain keeps on the root or stem-word, as *man, man'ly, man'liness*; though in clustered words, with their first breath-sounds the same, the strain may shift for the sake of clearness, as 'Give me the *tea'*pot'—the tea*kettle* is given, and thereupon the bidder may say 'the teaPOT',' not the teaKETTLE.

In Greek the accent shifts in word-building, and likes mainly to settle at about two times or short breath-sounds from the end of the word; and in Welsh it settles mostly on the last breath-sound but one, as *eis'tedd*, a sitting; *eistedd'fod*, a sitting-stead; *eisteddfod'an*, sitting-steads, or bardic sessions.

Besides the word-strain (accent) and the speech-strain (emphasis), there is a speech-tuning (modulation) of the voice (voice-winding), which winds up or down with sundry feelings of the mind, and with question and answers and changes of the matter of speech.

Things may be *matterly* (concrete) or bodies of matter, as a *man*, a *tree*, a *stone*; or

Things may be *unmatterly* (abstract), not bodies of matter, as *faith, hope, love, shape, speed, emptiness*.

It is not altogether good that a matterly and unmatterly thing should be named by the very same word, as *youth*, a young man, and *youth*, youngness.

THINGS AND THING-NAMES.

Things are of many kinds, as a *man*, a *bird*, a *fish*; an *oyster*, a *sponge*, a *pebble*; *water, air, earth*; *honey, gold, salt*.

The names of things may be called Thing-names.

But there are one-head thing-names (proper names), the names each of some one thing of its kind; as *John*, the miller; *Toby*, the dog; *Moti*, the lady's Persian cat.

With Christian names may be ranked the so-called *patronymics*, or *sire-names*, taken from a father's name, as William *Johnson*, Thomas *Richardson*; or in Welsh, Enid Verch *Edeyrn*; or in Hebrew Jeroboam *Ben-nebat*.

Thing Sundriness and Thing Mark-words.

☞ *Mark* is here to be taken in its old Saxon meaning, *mearc*—what bounds, defines, describes, distinguishes.

The Welsh call the adjective the *weak name* or noun, *enw gwan*.

Sundriness of Sex, Kindred, Youngness, and Smallness.

Marked by sundry names or mark-words, or mark endings.

i. Sex.

The stronger or *carl* sex, as a *man*; the weaker or *quean* sex, as a *girl*; the *unsexly* things, as a *stone*.

Husband, wife.

Father, mother.

Brother, sister.

In Saxon the sexes in mankind were called *halves* or *sides*, the spear-half and the spindle-half.

Man, woman.

Boy, girl.

Buck, doe.

Stag, hind.

Ram, ewe.

Cock, hen.

He-goat, *she-goat*.

King, queen.

Duke, duchess.

ii. Kindred, Youngness, or Smallness.

Father, son.

Mother, daughter.

Mare, foal.

Hind, fawn.

Cat, kitten.

Duck, duckling.

Goose, gosling.

Ethel, ethelin g.

iii. Small Things.

By forlessening mark-endings:

-y, -ie.

Lass, lassie.

Dog, doggie.

-kin.

Man, mannikin.

-el, -l.

Butt, bottle (of hay).

Pot, pottle.

Nose, nozzle.

By mark-words:

A *wee* house, a *little* boy.

For bigness the English tongue wants name-shapes.

We have *bul, horse,* and *tom,* which are mark-words of bigness or coarseness.
- Bulfinch.
- Bullfrog.
- Bulhead (the Miller's Thumb. Pen-bwll, *Welsh*).
- Bulrush.
- Bulstang (the Dragonfly).
- Bullspink.

Horse.
- Bulltrout.
- Horse-bramble.
- Horse-chesnut.
- Horse-laugh.
- Horse-leech.
- Horse-mushroom.
- Horse-mussel.
- Horse-tinger.
- Horse-radish.

Tom.
- Tomboy.
- Tomcat.
- Tomfool.
- Tomnoddy.
- Tomtit.

The words *bul* and *horse* are not taken from the animals.

Sundriness in Tale.

By tale mark-words, as *one, five, ten*, and others onward.

Sundriness in Rank.

By rank-word, as *first, fifth, tenth, last*.

An, a, the so-called indefinite article, is simply the tale mark-word *an*, one.

Saxon,	an man.
Ger.,	ein mann.
West Friesic,	in.
East Friesic,	en.
Holstein,	en.
New Friesic,	ien.

We use *a* before a consonant, and *an* before a vowel, as *a* man, *an* awl. But it is not that we have put on the *n* to *a* against the yawning, but it is that the *n* has been worn off from *an*.

The Frieses and Holsteiners now say *ien man* and *en mann*.

The mark-word *an, a* is of use to offmark a common one-head name, as 'I have been to *a white church*' (common); or, without the mark-word, 'I have been to *Whitechurch*' (one-head), the name of a village so called. 'He lives by *a pool*'; 'he lives by *Pool*' (a town in Dorset). 'He works in *a broad mead*'; 'he works in *Broadmead*' (in Bristol).

As the Welsh has no such mark-word, it might be thought that it cannot give these two sundry meanings; and the way in which it can offmark them shows how idle it is to try one tongue only by another, or to talk of the unmeaningness or uselessness of the Welsh word moulding.

Llan-Tydno would mean *a church of Tydno*, but the parish called 'The Church of Tydno' is in Welsh *Llandydno*, which, as a welding of two words, hints to the Welsh mind that *Llandydno* is a proper name, and so that of a parish.

Hoel da would mean *a good Hoel*; but to Hoel, the good king, the Welsh gives as a welded proper name *Hoel dda*; and to *Julius Cæsar* the Welsh gives, as one welded proper name, *Iolo-voel*, Julius-bald, whereas *Iolo-moel* would mean some bald Julius.

One sundriness of tale, the marking of things under speech—as *onely* (singular) or *somely* (plural)—is by an onputting to the thing-name for *someliness* a mark-ending, or by a moulding of the name into another shape or sound.

By mark-endings, *-es, -s, -en, -n*.

Lash, lashes.

Cat, cats.

House, housen.

Shoe, shoon.

By for-moulding, as *foot, feet—tooth, teeth*; or by both word-moulding or sound-moulding and an ending, as *brother, brethren*.

When the singular shape ends in *-sh, -ss*, or *-x, -ks*, it takes on *-es* for the somely, as *lash, lashes; kiss, kisses; box, boxes*.

And surely, when the singular shape ends in *-st*, our Universities or some high school of speech ought to give us leave to make it somely by the old ending *-en* or *-es* instead of *-s*—*fist, fisten, fistes; nest, nesten, nestes*.

What in the world of speech can be harsher than *fists, lists, nests*?

It is unhappy that the old ending in *-en*, which is yet the main one in West Friesic, should have given way to the hissing *s*.

Where common names with the definite mark-word become names of places they are wont to lose the article, as *The Bath*, in Somerset, is now *Bath*; *The Wells*, in Somerset, *Wells*; *Sevenoaks*, not *The Seven Oaks*, in Kent.

In our version of Acts xxvii. 8, we have a place which is called *The Fair Havens*, instead of *Fairhavens* without the mark-word, as the Greek gives the name.

Other thing mark-words offmark all of the things of a name or set from others of another name or set.

All birds, or *all* the birds in the wood; or all taken singly, as *each* or *every* bird; or somely, as *set* or *share*; *some few* or *a few*; *many* or *a many* birds.

Another or *others* beyond one or some under speech.

Any one or *more* of a some, either apple or any apples.

Both, for the two without others; or

Much or *little* grass.

Many mark-words were at first thing-names.

Many was a *menge*, a main or upmingled set; and a great many men would mean a great set or gathering of men.

Few was *feo*, which seems to have meant at first a cluster or herd; and a few men was a few (cluster) of men.

Some was a *sam* or *som*, a set or upmingled mass; and *some* men was a *sam* or *som* of men.

Now if the speech is about the set, it may be onely, as 'There *is* a great many,' 'there *is* a small few,' or 'a few'; but if the speech is about the bemarked things, the mark-word may well be somely—'many men *are*'; 'few men *are*'; 'some men *are*.'

In the queer wording, 'many a man,' 'many a flow'r is born to blush unseen,' it is not at all likely that *a* is the article. It is rather a worn shape, like *a* in *a-mong* (an-menge), or *a-hunting* (an-huntunge), of the Saxon case-word *an* or *on*, meaning *in*; and it is not unlikely that *man* has, by the mistaking of *a* for an article, taken the stead of *men*—'an maeng an men,' a many or mass in men; as we say 'a herd in sheep,' 'a horde in gold.' So far as this is true the mark-word may be somely—'many a man or men,' 'a main in men *are*.'

None (Saxon *na-an*, no one) should have a singular verb—'None *is* (not *are*) always happy.'

Some mark-words are for a clear outmarking (as single or somely) of things outshown from among others.

Outshowing Mark-words.

(Near things.)

Single.   Somely.
This man.   *These* men.

(Farther off.)

That. *Those.*

(Still farther off, or out of sight.)

Yon.

The so-called definite article *the* is a mark-word of the same kind as *this, that, these,* and *those.*

The word *the* in 'the more the merrier' is not the article *the*—to a name-word. It is an old Saxon outshowing mark-word meaning with that (*mid þy*). 'The more the merrier'; *þy* (with that measure), they are more; *þy* (with that measure), they are merrier.

In the wording 'the man *who*' or 'the bird *which* was in the garden,' *who* and *which* are not the names, but are tokens or mark-words of the things—*who* of the *man,* and *which* of the *bird.*

A thing may be marked by many mark-words, as 'the (never to be forgotten) day,' 'the (having to me shown so many kindnesses) man is yet alive.'

A long string of mark-words may, however, be found awkward, and so we may take a name-token *who* for the *man,* and, instead of the words 'having to me shown so many kindnesses,' say, 'who showed me so many kindnesses.'

Who or *that* is the name-token for menkind, and *which* or *that* for beings of lower life or of no life, as 'the man *who*' or 'the bird or flower *which* was in the garden.'

Who and *which* are used in the asking of questions—'*Who* is he?' '*What* is that?'

The name-token should follow close on the forename for the sake of clearness. 'Alfred sold, for a shilling, the *bat which* William gave him,' not 'Alfred sold the bat for a *shilling which* William gave him,' if it was the *bat* that was given to him by William.

These mark-words take the stead of thing-names, and are *Name-stead words,* and clear the speech of repetitions of the names. The baby may say 'Baby wants the doll,' but at length learns to say '*I* want the doll'; or '*Papa,* take *baby,*' and afterwards '*You* take *me*'; or 'Give *baby* the *whip*—the *whip* is *baby's,*' for '*It* is *mine.*'

A man may be beholden to the speech in three ways:—

- (1) He may be the speaker, called the First Person;
- (2) He may be spoken to, the Second Person (the to-spoken thing);
- (3) He may be spoken of, the Third Person (the of-spoken thing);

and some mark-words are for the marking of things without their names, both in tale and their sundry beholdenness to the speech:—

Single. Somely.

1st Person.

I. We.

2nd Person.

*Thou Ye,
. you.*

3rd Person.

He, she, it.

Here the sex is marked.

It is sometimes put for an unforeset thing-name of an unbodily cause or might, as '*it* rains'; '*it* freezes.'

For a child or an animal of unknown sex we may take the neuter (or sexless) mark-word *it*. '*It* (the child) cries.'

SUCHNESS OR QUALITIES,

and mark-words or mark-wording of suchness, as *good, bad, long, heavy*.

Suchness may be marked by one word, as 'a *white* lily,' or by a some or many of words, as 'a *very white* lily,' or 'a *most dazzlingly white* lily,' or 'a lily as *white as snow*.'

Things are marked as having much of something, as *hilly, stony, watery*; or made of something, as *golden, wooden, woollen*; or having some things, as *two-legged, three-cornered, long-eared*, or *loved* or *hated*; of the same set or likeness of something, as *lovely, quarrelsome, manly, childish*; wanting of something, as *beardless, friendless*.

Pitches of Suchness.

The Suchnesses of Things are of sundry pitches, which are marked by sundry shapes or endings or bye-words of the mark-words, as 'My ash is *tall*, the elm is *taller*, and the Lombardy poplar is the *tallest* of the three trees'; or 'Snow is *whiter* than chalk,' or 'Chalk is *less white* than snow,' or 'John is the *tallest* or *least tall* of the three brothers.'

These Pitch-marks offmark sundry things by their sundry suchnesses, as 'The *taller* or *less tall* man of the two is my friend,' or 'The *tallest* man is *less tall* than the tree,' or 'The *least tall* man is *taller* than the girl.'

The three Pitches may be called the *Common Pitch*, the *Higher Pitch*, and the *Highest Pitch*.

The Welsh has a fourth Pitch-word, called the *Even Pitch*, as *pell*, far; *pellach*, farther; *pellaf*, farthest; *pelled*, as far (as something else).

Younger may mean *younger* reckoned from young, or *younger* reckoned from *old*; as 'Alfred at 80 is younger than Edward at 85.' In this case we may well say *less old*.

Worse (wyrse) is shapen from *wo*, *wa*, *we*, a stub-root which means *wrong*, *atwist*, *bad* in any way, and is our *woe*.

The *r* in *weor* is most likely of a forstrengthening and not a comparative meaning—*weor*, *wyr*, very bad; *weorer*, *wyrer*, still more strongly bad. But, not to double the *r*, men might have put a strengthening *s*, and so had *weors*.

TIME-TAKING.

You cannot behold a thing in your mind otherwise than in or under some doing or in some form of being.

Every case of being or doing is a taking of time, as 'the lily *is* white,' 'the man *strikes*,' 'the bird *flies* or *was hit*.' For though the *being* white, or the *striking* or *flying* or *hitting* was only for the twinkling of an eye, it took time; for the eyelid takes time, however short it may be, to flit down and up over the eyeball. Thence the word commonly called the *verb* may be called the *Time-taking word* or *Time-word*, as it is called by the Germans *Das Zeitwort*; or, as it is the main word of the thought and speech, it is the *Thought-word* or *Speech-word*; or, as it is called in Latin and other tongues, the *Word*.

Welsh speech-lore has called the verb the *soul*[1] of the thought-wording.

Among the thousands of sundriness of time-taking there are some wide differences which should be borne in mind.

Unoutreaching or Intransitive.

Time-takings, which must or may end with the time-taking thing, as

To be. John cannot *be* another man.

To sleep; *to walk.* John cannot *sleep* or *walk* another man.

Outreaching (Transitive).

Time-takings that may begin with the time-taking thing, and reach out to another, as

To strike; *to see.* John may *strike* or *see* another man.

Time-giving.

If a man, A, takes time against another, B, as *to see* B, we should more truly say of B that he *gives*, not *takes*, the time which A takes.

The time-words for unoutreaching time-takings may be called *Unoutreaching*; of the outreaching ones, *Outreaching*; of the time-givings, *Time-giving*.

In some cases there is between the time-taking thing and the time-giving thing a middle one—the thing, tool, or matter with which the time is taken, as 'John hit William *with* a stone' or 'a cane.' But then, again, this wording is shortened by the putting of the name of the mid-thing as a time-word, as 'John *stoned* or *caned* William.' And this brings in a call for the marking of two sundry kinds of time-words—the strong or moulded, and weak or unmoulded time-words.

A time-word, when it tells a taking of time by one thing against another, is in the outreaching (active) *voice*—'John strikes the iron.' When it tells of the giving of time, it is in the time-giving (passive) *voice*. When it tells of an unoutreaching time-taking it is in the middle *voice*.

For the causing of another thing to take time some tongues have set shapes of the time-word, as, in Hindustani, *durna*, to run; *durāna*, to make another run.

We have hardly any of such words, though such are—
- Lie, lay.
- Sit, set.
- Rise, raise.

Time-takings for becoming or making another thing become otherwise are marked by the ending *-en* on the mark-word, as
- To blacken.
- To whiten.

Misdoing by the fore-eking *mis-*:—
- Mistake.
- Misread.

Longer-lasting time-takings marked by the ending *-er*, as

Chat, chatter (to chatter much or long).

Fret, fritter.

Sway, swagger.

Short or *small time-takings* by endings such as *-ock, -ick*.

Whinne, whinnock whinnick (to whine smally).

-el, -l.

Pratle, prattle.

Jog, joggle.

16

Crack, crackle.

A time-taking, taken as a deed or being without any time-taking thing, is taken as a *thing*, and its name is a *Thing-name*, as *to write*.

As in Greek the Infinitive mood, *tò gráphein*, the 'to write'; and in Italian, *il scrivere*, the 'to write' (the deed of writing or a writing), so the Infinitive mood-shape of the Saxon time-word was taken as a thing-name after the preposition *to*, to or for, as *to huntianne* (to or for the deed to hunt or hunting), as 'Why does Alfred keep those dogs?' 'To huntianne.'

Thence we have our wording—
- 'Any chairs *to mend*?' (any chairs to or for the deed mending),
- 'A house *to let*,'
- 'Letters *to write*,'
- 'A tale *to tell*,'

which is all good English.

It is an evil to our speech that the thing-shape now ending in *-ing* should be mistaken for the mark-word ending in *-ing*.

Unhappily two sundry endings of the old English have worn into one shape. They were *-ung* or *-ing* and *-end*.

Singung is the deed of singing, a thing. *Singend* is a mark-word, as in the wording 'I have a *singing* bird.'

Sailing and *hunting*, in the foregiven thought-wordings, are thing-names, and not mark-words. *Sailing* is *segling*, as 'ne mid *seglinge* ne mid rownesse' (neither with sailing nor rowing).—Bede 5, 1.

'*Wunigende* ofer hyne' (*woning* [mark-word] over him).—Matt iii. 16.

'Sy *wunung* heora on west' (be their *woning* [thing-name] waste).—Ps. lxviii 30.

'Ða genealaehton hym to Farisaer hyne *costigende*' (then came near to him the Pharisees *tempting* [mark-word] him).—Matt xix. 3.

'Ne gelaede þu us on *costnunge*' (lead us not into *tempting* [thing-name]).—Lord's Prayer.

So 'haelende,' Matt v. 23; 'haeling'; 'bodigende,' Matt. x. 35; 'bodung,' Luke xi. 32.

'Waere þu to-daeg, on huntunge?' (not *huntende*) (wert thou to-day on or in hunting?)—Aelfric's Dialogue.

'Hwaet dest þu be þinre huntunge?' (not *huntende*) (what dost thou by thy hunting?)—Aelfric.

'*The* CALLING *of* assemblies I cannot away with.'—Isa. i. 13. Not 'calling assemblies,' which, if *calling* were a mark-word, would mean assemblies that call.

The right speech-trimming with the thing-names in *-ing* is to trim them in the old English way as thing-names in their cases; as,

'We are the *offscouring* of all things unto this day.'—1 Cor. iv. 13. Not 'We are the offscouring all things.'

'For that righteous man, IN *seeing* and *hearing*, vexed his righteous soul.'

'By *the* WASHING *of* regeneration and (*the*) RENEWING *of* the Holy Ghost.'—Titus iii. 5. Not 'He saved us by the washing regeneration and renewing the Holy Ghost.'

The ending *-er* of the time-taker (*deeder*, name-word) is, not unclearly, the Celtic, Welsh *gwr*, or in word-welding *-wr*, the Latin *-or*; as,

Welsh, *barn*, doom; *barnwr*, a doom-man.
Latin, *canto*, to sing; *cantor*, a sing-man.

Thence *-er* seems a far less fitting ending for a tool-name than the old Saxon *-el*; and a tool for the whetting of knives would be more fitly called a *whettel* than a whetter. *Choppel*, chopper; *clippels*, clippers.

All new time-words now taken or shapen from other tongues must be unmoulded.

We say *shoot*, shot (not *shooted*); but *loot*, looted (not *lot*), *loot* being the Hindustani *lootna*, to rob or plunder.

So time-words, which are known English words, of another kind, names or mark-words, are mostly unmoulded.

The shapening of the time-words hangs rather more on their endings than on their headings.

The oddest are those which end in the throat-pennings—**NG, NK, K, G**; and those ending in roof-pennings—**T, D**.

Because the *-d* of the roof-penning *-ed* is so unlike a throat-penning, which cannot easily stand with it: and because the **T** and **D** are like *d* as roof-pennings, and (*see* Table) they may run into them.

-ING Root-words (strong).

The wording of a time-taking (predicate) with its speech-thing (subject) is a *Thought-wording* (proposition).

Strong or *moulded time-words* are such as, for a time-taking of foretime, are moulded (without any out-eking) into another shape or sound, as

I   I
sing, sang.

It   it
flies, flew.

The *weak* or *unmoulded time-words* take on, unmoulded, an ending such as *-ed*, as

He   he
stones, stoned.

He canes, he *caned.*

All time-words that are known names of things are unmoulded, as

Too Plaster, plastered.

Bud, budded.

Comb, combed.

Cap, capped.

Dust, dusted.

Fish, fished.

Gate, gated.

Water, watered.

Heap, heaped.

Mind, minded.

Name, named.

Pen, penned.

Stone, stoned.

Very many of our time-words are unmoulded from the same cause—that they are names of things; although such names of things, having become worn more or less out of shape, or having fallen out of use, may not show themselves to our minds what they are.

To hunt makes *hunted*; why? From *hound*, to hunt, meaning at first to seek with a hound.

It may, however, be said, 'Is to hunt from *hound*, or hound from *to hunt?*'

Such a point is, in very many cases, cleared out by the Anglo-Saxon, in which 'to hunt' is *hunt-i-an*, not *hunt-an*; and the *i*, a worn shape of *ig*, shows that *huntian* is from *hund*, hound, and so hound is not from hunt.

The time-word from the thing *hunt-ig-an, hunt-i-an*, is to *houndy*, to take time with a hound.

We say

Cling, clung.

Fling, flung.

Sling, slung.

But we should say 'he *ringed* (not rung) his pig'; 'he *stringed* his harp'; *ring* and *string* being *things*.

The *strong* or *moulded time-words* are nearly or quite all words ending in one single breath-penning, and of a close sound (1, 2, 3, or 4 of the Table), as

ING, - , Cling, clung.

INK, - Sink, sank.

-K, Speak, spoke.

-L, Steal, stole.

-T, Smite, smote.

-R, Tear, tore.

-V, Weave, wove.

Other time-words, name-words, or stem-words, and broad-sounded ones (5, 6, 7, 8 of the Table), are nearly all weak or unmoulded.

Weak.

The ending **-NG** in broad-sounded words—

Clang, clanged.

Bung, bunged.

Long, longed.

-NK, Broad.

Bank, banked.

Clank, clanked.

Flank, flanked.

And in

Blink, blinked.

Link, linked.

Clink, clinked.

-K, Broad, Long Stem-words (weak).

Bake, baked.

Croak, croaked.

Hawk, hawked.

Rake, raked.

Make was heretofore *maked*:
'For aevric rice man his castles *makede*.'—Sax. Chron. MCXXXVI.
K wore out, whence

21

Maked, ma-ed, maed, made.

-K, Short.

Back, backed.

Clack, clacked.

-G, Short.

Beg, begged.

Clog, clogged.

All but *dig*, dug. What a pity to put it out of keeping with all of the others! It is *digged* in the Bible.

-T, Long Stem-words.

Bait, baited.

Bate, bated.

Bleat, bleated.

Bloat, bloated.

Clout, clouted.

Float, floated.

-T, Short Stem-words.

Bat, batted.

Bet, betted.

Cl clotte

ot, d.

-TH.

Breathe, breathed.

-T, Short (weak shortened).

Cut, cut.

Hit, hit.

Let, let.

Set, set.

&c.

The wear of these words was thislike:
- Let-*ede*.
- Let-*de*.

The mild penning, *d*, after a hard one, *t*, became hard, *t*. Whence *lette*, let, with the two *tt run into one*. A pity!

So were shapen *feed, fedde, fed; lead, ledde, led; read, redde.*

Weak -D (long).

Crowd, crowded.

Fade, faded.

Weak -D (short).

Bed, bedded.

Bud, budded.

-L, Broad Sound (long).

Brawl, brawle

wl, d.

Call, called.

A few of them are shortened, as *feel, feeld, felt*.

-N, Long.

Clean, cleaned.

Frown, frowned.

-N, Short Stem-words.

Din, dinned.

Pin, pinned.

Sin, sinned.

-R, Broad Sounds.

Blare, blared.

Care, cared.

Dare now makes *durst*; but in Friesic it is unmoulded—'and ne *thuradon* nâ wither forskina' (and *dared* not to show themselves again).

-R, Short.

Bar, barred.

Purr, purred.

Stir, stirred.

-S and -Z, Long.

Pose posed

Praise,	praised.
Blaze,	blazed.
Close,	closed.
Daze,	dazed.
Raze,	razed.

-SS.

Bless,	blessed.
Guess,	guessed.

-SH.

Blush,	blushed.
Clash,	clashed.

-P, Long.

Heap,	heaped.
Peep,	peeped.
Reap,	reaped.
Gape,	gaped.
Cope,	coped.

Hope,	hoped.
Mope,	moped.
Stoop,	stooped.
Weak.	Shortened.
Creep,	crep'd.
Keep,	kep'd.
Leap,	lep'd.
Sleep,	slep'd.
Weep,	wep'd.
Sweep,	swep'd.

-P, Short.

Cap,	capped.
Hap,	happed.
Hop,	hopped.
Stop,	stopped.

Weak -B (short).

Blab, blabbed.

-V, Long.

Crave, craved.

Grave, graved.

Rave, raved.

-F, Short.

Huff, huffed.

Cough, coughed.

-M, Long.

Blame, blamed.

All but *come*, came.

Stub-roots.

Time-words ending in an open breathing. Most of them are weak:—

Bay, bayed.

Bow, bowed.

Brew, brewed.

Claw, clawed.

Say, said.

Stew, stewed.

A few of them are moulded:—

Blow,	blew.
Crow,	crew.
Grow,	grew.
Slay,	slew.

All those that end in two or three sundry breath-pennings are weak:—

-NCH,	Pinch,	pinched.
-ND,	Land,	landed.
-NGE,	Lounge,	lounged.
-NT,	Grant,	granted.
-PL,	Cripple,	crippled.
-PT,	Intercept,	intercepted.
-RB,	Barb,	barbed.
-RC,	Cork,	corked.
-RD,	Hord,	horded.
-RG,	Charge,	charged.
-RL,	Hurl,	hurled.
-BL,	Bubble,	bubbled.
-CL,	Cackle,	cackled.

-DL,	Huddle,	huddled.
-FL,	Ruffle,	ruffled.
-FT,	Heft,	hefted.
-GL,	Naggle,	naggled.
-LP,	Gulp,	gulped.
-LK,	Chalk,	chalked.
-LD,	Mould,	moulded.
-LP,	Help,	helped.
-LV,	Calve,	calved.
-MB,	Climb,	climbed.
-MP,	Pump,	pumped.
-MT,	Tempt,	tempted.
-RM,	Harm,	harmed.
-RN,	Burn,	burned.
-RP,	Carp,	carped.
-RT,	Flirt,	flirted.
-RTH,	Earth,	earthed.
-SS,	Miss,	missed.
-SP,	Clasp,	clasped.
-ST,	Consist,	consisted.

(All but *cast*, formerly *casted*.)

-TCH, Hatch, hatched.

-TL, Bottle, bottled.

-RST, Burst, bursted.

A few time-words ending with a throat-penning mark the heretofore time by some oddness of shape; as,

Bring, brought.

Think, thought.

They were opened in sound, and also took the ending *ode, od* (our *ed*), and then came into our shapes by sundry wonted changes:—

-*ing* (as of *bring*) became -*ong*.

-*ing*-ed	became	(1) -*ong*-ed.
-*ong*-ed	"	(2) -*ong'd*.
-*ong'd*	"	(3) -*onk'd*.

Then the *d*, a mild penning after a hard penning (*k*), became hard, *t*:—

-*onk'd*	became	(4) -*onk't*.
-*onk't*	"	(5) -*ok't*.
-*ok't*	,,	(6) -*o't*,

as *k* and *t* are harsh together. Whence—

Bring   bro't

	(brought).
Buy (*bycg*, A.S.)	bo't.
Seek (*sec*, A.S.)	so't.
Teach (*taec*, A.S.)	to't.

Our *gh* as in *taught* is the now unuttered (though still written) throat-penning.

Time-takings or time-givings may be taken as thing-marks, as 'the *hunting* dog'; 'the *hunted* hare.'

The sundry moods of time-takings are marked by sundry shapes of the time-word, or by bye-words or mark-words—*shall, will, can, may, must.*

The timings of time-takings are marked by sundry shapes of the time-word, and by bye-words or mark-words to it, as 'the bird flies' or does fly, or flew or did fly, or will fly.

Under-Sundrinesses of Time-takings.

Time-takings are of sundry kinds, under sundry names, as *to be, to walk, to strike.*

Under-time-markings may be by single words, as 'to write *well* or *ill, slowly* or *quickly*'; or by two or three words, as 'he runneth *very swiftly*'; or by clusters of words, as 'he runs *with most amazing speed*'; or 'he works *in a very skilful way.*'

Fitting of the Time-word to all the cases of Person, Time, and Mood.

In this fitting the time-word is helped by sundry bye-words or under-mark-words.

Can, from the Saxon *cun-n-an*, to ken, know, to know how. 'I *can* write,' I know how to write.

The heretofore time-shape of *Ic can* was *Ic cuðe*, for which we have now *I could*, with an *l* which was never in the root of the word, and for which there is not any ground.

May.—*Mag-an*, the stem of *maht*, *might*, means *to strongen*, to be or become strong (Lat. *valere*), as is shown by cases of its use in Saxon and other Teutonic tongues.

In an old Friesic good wish at the drinking to the health of a bride and bridegroom we find 'Dat se lang lave en wel mage,' that they long live and well *may* (*strongen, bene valeant*); and in Saxon, 'Hu maeg he?' how mays he? (*strongens* or *valet*).

Shall.—*Sceal-an*, meant, as a stem, to offmark, distinguish, or to *skill* in the meaning of 1 Kings v. 6—'Ic sceal dón,' I offmark or skill to do; as what I am bent to do.

'Thou shalt love the Lord thy God.' Thou markest or clearly seest to love the Lord thy God.

'Thou shalt not steal.' Thou markest this. Not to steal.

Must.—*Mot-an, most-an,* is most likely a stem of the word *mag-an,* to strongen (*valere*).

The *-st* would strengthen the meaning of *mag* (may) as it does in *-est* of *longest.* So 'I must go' (Ic moste gán) would mean 'I am overmighted by another's might to go.'

Time-words are fitted

To *Person,* as

I am.   Thou art.   He is.

To *Tale,* as

I am.   Thou art.   He is.
We are.   Ye are.   They are.

To *Time,* as

I am (now).   I was (heretofore).

I shall be (hereafter).

To *Mood,* as

I write, or shall write.
I may or can write, or might or could or should write.
If I write, or if I had written.

Things and Time-takings.

Timing of time-takings is the marking of their times, as *now, heretofore,* or *hereafter.*

Time.

Now or *hereat.*
I am, or I love, or am loved.

Heretofore done.
I was, or I loved, or was loved.

Heretofore ongoing.
I was, or I was a-loving or I did love.

Now ended.
I have been, or I have loved, or have been loved.

Heretofore ended.
I had been, or I had loved, or had been loved.

Heretofore ongoing, ended.
I had been a-loving.

Hereafter doing.
I shall be, or I shall love, or shall be loved.

Hereafter ongoing.
I shall be a-loving.

Hereafter ended.
I shall have been, or shall have loved, or shall have been loved.

Hereafter ended, ongoing.
I shall have been a-loving.

Single and stringly time-takings of the same name, as 'Mary *sold* me some apples yesterday.' There was a single selling; but under the wording 'Mary formerly *sold* apples in the market,' it is clear that under the same word *sold* is meant a string of sellings.

So under the wording '*Write* your name' is understood a single writing; but under the wording 'If you would write readily, write every day,' the same word *write* implies a string of writings.

Some tongues (as the Greek and Russian) have two shapes of the time-words for these two cases of time-taking; as, Greek—

'Take thy bill and write fifty' (γράψον, *aorist*).—Luke xvi. 6.

'Jesus, stooping down, wrote on the ground' (ἔγραφεν, *imperfect*, ondoing shape, *wrote on*).

But Acts xxv. 26, 'About whom I have nothing certain to write' (γράψαι, *aorist*, to write off once for all).

See the Greek text of the 3rd Epistle of John v. 13—'I had many (things or many times?) to *write* (γράφειν, ondoing shape), but I will not with pen and ink *write* (γράψαι) to thee' (*aorist*, offdoing form).

An understanding of the difference between the *aorist* and ondoing shapes is of weight in the reading of the Gospel. 'To *make intercession*, to *intercede* for them.'—Heb. vii. 25. To intercede once for all, at the doom-day? No. To intercede on always; for the word is not in the *aorist* shape, but in the present ondoing form, *to be interceding*.

Historic Time-wording.

A time-shape of a time-word used in an unwonted way for the telling of a string of deeds, as, in English, the present time-shape is so used for deeds of foretime, as 'He *opens* the door, *walks* in, coolly *takes* a chair, *sits* down, and *tells* the maid he wishes to see me.'

So 'Philip *findeth* Nathanael, and *saith* unto him,' &c.—John i. 45.

The Moods of Time-takings.

Mood.

The wording of the time-taking may be; as,

(1) Now or heretofore true, or hereafter sure, as 'He *is*, or *was*, or *will be*'; 'He *sings*, or *sang*, or *will sing*.' *The Truth Mood.*

(2) That it may or can, or could or might be so taken, as 'He may or can go.' *The Mayly Mood.*

(3) Or that it is to be wished that it may or might be taken, as 'I wish,' or 'Oh that I could go.' *The Wish Mood.*

Or that it is a hinge time-taking on which another hangs, as 'If you ask (hinge), you will receive (on-hang).'

Or as bidden to be taken, as 'Go thy way.'

Stead-marks and Way-marks of Time-takings.

Case.

Things named in speech, so as to mark the stead of the beginning or end, or of the way of the time-taking at any point of its length or outreach in time or room, are Case-things.

There are, however, two cases which are speech-cases and not stead-marks or way-marks:—

(1) That of the of-spoken thing (nominative), the thing of which the speech speaks, as 'The bird flies'; and

(2) The to-spoken thing (vocative), as 'O sing, sweet bird.'

Cases are marked by shapes of thing-names or by case-words, or by the setting of the case-word either after or before the time-word, as 'The dog drove out the cat,' where the dog is the beginning of the time-taking; or 'The cat drove out the dog,' where the dog is the end of it, and is shown to be so by the setting of its name after the time-word.

                                                          iv.   **Source.**

'The bird flew from, or off, or out of the *tree*.'

'He died of or from *intemperance*.'

The *tree* and *intemperance* are source-marks of *flew* and *died*.

                                                           v.   **End or Aim.**

'John loved *George*.'

'He went to or towards *London*.'

'Edwin worked for *wages*, or strolled along by the *stream*.'

          vi. **The Stead Case.**

'John was in the *field* or at the *church*.'

          vii. **The Tool.**

'Alfred wrote with a *pen*.'

'The bird flew before, behind, over, under, above, below, by, around, or through the *gate-turret*,' which is the way-mark of *flew*.

There is a Source-mark which is a source of the time-taking, not as being only that thing, but as being a thing then in some shape or kind of time-taking.

'(*a*) The wind being against us, (*b*) we made but little way.' *a* is the source of *b*, 'we made but little way,' not from the wind simply as wind, but as also being against us.

'You being my leader, I shall overcome.'

This is commonly called the absolute case (allfree case); though the wind is not free of a time-taking (being against us). It may be called the 'thing-so-being' case.

Some tongues mark many of the cases by sundry endings of the thing-name, but we have in common names only one ending for case, the possessive, as 'the horse's mane,' 'John's house.'

In name-tokens we have three case-forms, as *thou*, *thy*, *thee*—*thy* for the possessive, and *thee* for all the other cases.

'The bird flew *from* the apple-tree *in* the corner *of* the garden, *through* the archway, and *under* the elm *by* the barn, *round* the hayrick, and on *over* the stream just *below* the willow, and *above* the bridge, and then *to* the stall, and on *towards* the wood, and *into* an ivy-bush.'

Here the sundry named things are way-marks which mark the place of the *flying* in its beginning and end, and at sundry points of its length.

Such stead-marks or way-marks may be taken as in either of one or two or three cases, as they may be either stead-marks or way-marks, and as their beholdingness to the time-taking may be reckoned to it or from it to themselves.

'The bird flew *over* or *under* or *by* the tree.' The flying at first reached on nearer towards the tree, and then reached off again farther from it, so that the tree was at first in the case of a toness, and then in the case of a fromness, with the flying.

But under the wording 'the roof is *over* the floor,' or 'the floor is *under* the roof,' the time-taking *is* is a staid and not an ongoing one, and either the roof or the floor may be in the fromness or toness case, as the height may be reckoned from it to the other, or to it from the other.

A housemother may say 'We live near (*to*) Fairton' (toness case); yet an hour afterwards she may say 'We live too far *from* Fairton (fromness case) to step in readily for errands.'

Her abode may be four miles from Fairton, so that the time-taking *live* is as far from Fairton in one case as the other; and yet it puts it in two sundry cases.

'If Alfred gave to Edred a field,' the time-taking *gave* ended in the mid-thing, the field (the endingness case), but it put the field to Edred, as his, in the toness case.

The place of a time-taking may be shown by one place-mark, or by two or three, of which a latter may mark the place of a former, as 'The rooks build *in* the elms, *above* the house,' where the elms mark the place of the *building*, and the house marks that of the place-mark (the *elms*).

But some case-words are made up of a smaller case-word and a thing-name, as 'Alfred sat *beside* the wall.' *Beside* being 'by the *side*,' and the side of the wall (whereof case).

The figure for *case-shifting*, or the changing of the case-tokens, is called in Gr. *enallage* as

'I have ten sovereigns *in my purse*'; '*My purse* contains ten sovereigns.'

'*The pump has* a new handle'; 'There is a new handle *to the pump*.'

'The carpet *in* the hall'; 'The carpet *of* the hall.'

'The brother *of* or *to* that lady.'

'John *likes* cricket or is *fond of* cricket.'

'Greedy *of* gain or *for* gain.'

'Think *of* me or *on* me.'

'He was killed by a blow *of a club* or *with a club*.'

'He spoke *in* the balcony or *from* the balcony.'

THOUGHT-WORDING, SPEECH-WORDING,

is the setting of words or a bewording of thought or speech (syntax).

A thought-wording (proposition) is a bewording of the case of a thing with its time-taking. 'The boy is good' or 'the boy plays.'

A thought-wording may have more thing-names and time-words, as 'The boys and girls read and play.'

Thought-wordings (propositions) may be linked together in sundry ways, though mostly by Link-words (conjunctions). 'Men walk *and* birds fly'; 'I sought him, *but* I found him not'; 'I waited at the door *while* Alfred went into the house.'

Twin Time-takings.

The *Hinge* Time-taking, on which the other hangs, and the *Hank* Time-taking which hangs on the Hinge one, as 'If ye ask (*hinge*), ye shall receive (*hank*).'

There are sundry kinds of hinge time-takings, as one or the other or both of the time-takings may or may not be trowed or true or sure.

(1) *Hinge* and *hank*, trowed—'As ye ask (as I trow you do), so ye receive (I trow).'

(2) *Hinge*, untrowed; *hank*, trowed—'If ye ask (I trow not whether ye will or no), then ye will receive (I trow).'

The hinge-word put down as trowedly untrue, and the hank one trowed, as 'If ye asked (as I trow you do not), ye would receive (I trow)'; or 'If ye had asked (ye have not), ye would have received (I trow).'

The hinge time-taking trowed, and the other untrowed, as 'Ye ask (I trow), that ye may receive (I trow not that ye will).'

Speech-trimming.

The putting of speech into trim; *trim* being a truly good form or state. To *trim* a shrub, a bonnet, or a boat, is to put it into trim.

1. The first care in speech-trimming is that we should use words which give most clearly the meanings and thoughts of our mind, though it is not likely that unclear thought will find a clear outwording; and either of the two, as clear or unclear, helps to clearen or bemuddle the other.

With most English minds, and with all who have not learned the building of Latin and Greek words, English ones may be used with fewer mistakes of meaning than would words from those tongues; though Englishmen should get a clearer insight into English word-building ere they could hope to keep English words to their true sundriness of meaning.

The so-seeming miswordings (solœcisms) of writers in the Latinised and Greekish speech-trimming are not uncommon or unmarkworthy.

One man writes of something which *necessitates* another, though Latin itself has no *necessito* to back 'necessitate'; another gives *eliminate* as meaning *elicit*, or outdraw; a third calls a *failure* of a rule an *exception* from it. There is no EXCEPTION to a rule but that which is *excepted* from it at and in the downlaying of it. If a man gives a simple rule 'that if it rains on St. Swithin's day it rains forty days after it,' and it did not so rain last year, the case is a *breach* or *failure* of the rule, and not an *exception* to it. He gave no exception.

Some say 'Mrs. A. has had *twins*' or 'Alfred was one of *twins*.' A twin is a *twain*, a *two*, or a couple of things of the same name or kind; and twins of children must be at least four. I should say 'Alfred was one of *a* twin.' In the latter case it would be correct to say 'There IS *one* or a *twain* of fat men,' &c., in which *is* would match both.

One has written 'ideas are *manufactured*.' By whose hands? Another talks of 'a *dilapidated* dress'; and a third has 'found the stomach of a big fish *dilapidated*.' What are *lapides*? and what means *delapido*?

A man has written of an old Tartar that he was 'a *tameless* gorilla'—a gorilla without a *tame*! as if *tame* were a thing-name.

Another says 'It imposed *absolute limits* upon the choice of positions.' What are *absolute limits* if absolute (from *absolvo*, to offloosen) means offloosened from all check and all limits?

A man writes of 'a photograph reproduced by a new permanent process.' Is it the process or the sunprint that is permanent?

Preposterous, foreaft, as when what should be *præ*, foremost, is put *post* or behind; whereas a writer gives a structure as 'preposterously overgrown,' as if 'preposterous' meant only very much, vastly.

One takes *irretrievable* as nohow amended. If 'retrieve' is the French *retrouver* (to find again), 'irretrievable' would mean not to be found again; and 'the irretrievable defeat of the whole nation' would be one which they could not *find* again, as most likely they would not wish to find it.

Twy-meanings.

From want of words in English, or of care, our wording may seem to bear two meanings, as 'John played with Edwin, and broke his bat.' The bat of which boy?

'One Robert Bone of Antony shot at a little bird sitting upon his cow's back, and killed it—the bird (I mean), not the cowe.'—*Carew.*

Word-sameness (Synonyms).

Words of the same meaning are less often so than they are so called; and we sometimes give lists of synonyms showing the differences of their meanings.

A twin of words of one very same meaning is rather evil than good; and if they are not of one very same meaning they should not be given as such.

It may be that from a misunderstanding of the word *tautology*, as the name of a bad kind of speech-trimming, men have often shunned the good use of words.

The bad tautology from which speakers have been so frayed seems to be the giving twice or many times, within one scope of thought-wording, the same matter of speech in the same words.

It is true that it would not be good wording to say 'John has sold *John's* horse' for '*his* horse' since the name-tokens are shapen to stand for foregiven names.

But where the same foreused word would give a very clear—if not the clearest—meaning, there seems to be little ground against the use of it.

'I bought a horse on Monday and a donkey on Tuesday, and sold the *horse* again at a gain on Thursday.' Why should not the word *horse* take the latter place as well as the word *steed*, or equine animal, or 'more worthy beast'—or why should I not as well say, 'An ass I want, and an ass I will buy,' as 'An ass I want, and a donkey, or *it* or *him*, I will buy'?

It seems that much wrong is done to the Greek of the Gospel by the putting, for the same Greek word, sundry English ones at sundry passages; and by what right do we try an Evangelist's or an Apostle's wisdom in the use of the same word, by which he must have meant to give the same meaning? or why should we make him to mean by κρίσις, at one time, a trying of a soul, and at another time a fordooming of him?

It is not any tautology to use near to each other a thing-name and a mark-word which are only fellow stem-words, as 'As *free*, and not using your *freedom* for a cloke of wickedness.'

2. Another care in speech-trimming is the choice of words for their sound-sweetness (Gr. *euphony*) or well-soundingness, or for speech-readiness.

Past, with the hissing *s* with *t*, is less sound-good than *after*; and *aqueduct*, with *ct*, is less well-sounding than *waterlode*; nor is *cataract* softer than *waterfall*.

The hereunder given wordings were lately heard in a law court:—

'I can give you *one or two instances* of remarkable intelligence in the cases of fat men'; and

A Juror—'There *are one or two fat men* on the jury (laughter).'

Dr. K.—'I don't think there are.'

How should these cases be treated? In the first case, 'one instances' is a breach of word-matching, as would be 'two instance'; and in the latter, the word *one* calls for *man*, and *two* for *men*. May we not better say, 'I can give you at least one instance,' or 'I believe more instances than one'?

'A man who has already, and will still, render such services will be,' &c. *Rendered* is understood after *has*; but how may the thought be worded without the two puttings of the word *render*? Thus: 'a man who will still be, as he has already been, found to render,' &c.

Penetrate means insink, inpierce. M. Gambetta writes, 'After the heroic examples given by open towns, and by villages only guarded by their firemen, it is absolutely necessary that each town, each commune, shall pay its debt to the national defence, and that all alike be *penetrated* by the task which is imposed upon France.' It seems a queer speech-wording to take a *task* as a thing that *penetrates*, though it might be undertaken.

A bad wording is often found with mark-words of the higher pitch, as 'Alfred was more clever, but not so good, *as* John.' 'Not so good' is an inwedged word-cluster, but the word-setting is bad, as 'more clever' calls for the word *than*, not *as*; and 'so good' wants *as*, not *than*. It would be better to say 'Alfred was more clever, but less good, than John.' To try the word-setting take out the wedge-words ('but not so good'), and you will have 'Alfred was more clever *as* John.'

Dislike seems a bad word-shape. *Mislike* is the old and true English one. *Like* is from *lic*, a shape, as *lich*, the body of a dead man. 'It *liketh* (licað) me well' is 'it *shapes* itself (looketh) to me well.' 'It *misliketh* me' is 'it *misshapes* itself to me' (looks bad).

To *seem* is from the thing-name—*sam, seam, seem*, body or mass—and 'it *seems* to me' is 'it *bodies* itself to me.' 'That ship *seems* to be a French one,' or 'that man *seems* to be ill,' *bodies* itself or himself to be a French one or ill.

'The house and the goods *were* burnt'; but 'the house with the goods *was* (not *were*) burnt,' since it is only the house that is in the speech-case, as the goods are in the mate-case. 'The house *was* burnt with the goods.'

'*One* of the children *are* come.' No—*is* come. The one only is come.

In our taking of time-words from the Latin in the shape of the past participle, we get at last a queer shape of word. Take the Latin *reg-* of *rego*, to reach or straighten, as a line, and our word *reck*. From *reg* comes *regtus, rectus*. Here the *t* answers to our *d* (German *t* of *ed* and *et*). Then *rec-t* answers to *reck'd*. Now put on *ed* to each, and *rec-t* becomes *rec-t-ed*, as in *direc-t-ed*; and *reck'd* becomes *reck-d-ed*, showing that *directed* is truly *direg-ed-ed*, and too like *reck-ed-ed*, as 'He *reck-ed-ed* nought.'

We may often hear a man who is careful to speak good English say 'This rose smells very sweetly,' for sweet. The rose smells (gives out smell) as being itself very sweet, not as smelling (taking in smell) in a sweet way. To find which to use, the thing-markword or the under-markword, put '*as being*' after the time-word, as 'This rose smells (as being itself) *sweet*,' not sweetly.

'Can you smell now? you had, the other day, lost your smelling?' 'Yes, I smell very *nicely*.' Not I smell as being myself very *nice*. A rose cannot smell any other thing, and so cannot smell it *nicely*.

'Mary sings very *charmingly*,' but 'Mary looks very *charming*.'

'John looks *pale*,' but 'John looks very *narrowly* into that gold-work.'

'I can taste *well*,' 'That peach tastes *good*.'

To have seen a man at a bygone time would mean that the seeing was before that bygone time; but we sometimes hear a man say, 'I should (yesterday) have been very glad to have seen you (if you had called yesterday).' That is, by wording, 'I should have been very glad (yesterday) to have seen you (at a time before yesterday),' not to see you yesterday; and yet that is what the speaker means. 'I should have been very glad (yesterday) to see you (yesterday),' or 'I should be very glad to-day to have seen you yesterday.'

3. Odd word-shapes are not in the main choice-worthy.

Our time-word *go* is of unwontsome conjugation, as its foretime shape *went* is not shapen from *go*, but is a shape of another word, *wend*.

So the forlessening name, *leveret* for a *hareling*, and *cygnet* for a *swanling*, are unwontsome, as being words of another speech.

4. There is a greater or less freedom of *word-shifting* (Gr. *anastrophe*, up-shifting or back-shifting), as *up* in 'Fasten it *up* well,' 'fasten it well *up*'; or *back* in 'He brought *back* the saw,' or 'he brought the saw *back*'; 'There is none to dispute *my right*,' or '*my right* there is none to dispute.'

Why should not English, like other tongues, more freely form words with headings of case-words, as *downfalls, incomings, offcuttings, outgoings, upflarings*, instead of the awkward falls-down, comings-in, cuttings-off, goings-out, flare-ups; or *offcast* (for cast-off) clothes; or a *downbroken* (for a broken-down) schoolmaster; *outlock* or *outlocking* (for a lock-out); the *uptaking* beam (for the taking-up beam) of an engine?

Oddly-shapen or Oddly-taken Words.

Mongrel (hybrid) words, or words partly from one tongue and partly from another.

Twy-speechwords are a sore blemish to our English, as they seem to show a scantiness of words which would be a shame to our minds; as,

Sub-warder for under-warder.

Pseudo-sailor for sham-sailor.

Ex-king for rodless or crownless king.
Prepaid for forepaid.
Bi-monthly for fortnightly or every fortnight.

Wordiness (Verbosity).

As 'The train ran *with extraordinary velocity*,' for 'the train ran *very fast*.'

'Alfred did the business *with perfect fidelity*;' for 'Alfred did the business *faithfully*.'

Thence much of the wordiness of our written, if not spoken, composition.

The 'New York Times' thus explains how it was that the flames got to the roof in the burning of the Fifth Avenue Hotel:—'Fire always is aspirant, the sole exception being where incandescent masses fall down, and so act as a medium of ignition.'

The hard breathing (aspirate) is often wrongly dropped or misput by less good speakers; but, while the upper ranks laugh at them for their mistakes, they themselves, like our brethren of Friesland and Holstein, often drop it from words to which it of right belongs, and mainly from the hard-breathed **W** or the Saxon **HW** (our **WH**).

What	*wat* (Hols.)
When,	*wanne* (Fri.)
Where,	*wâr* (Fri.)
Wheel,	*weel* (Fri.)
Whelp,	*welp* (Fri.)
While,	*wile* (Fri.)
White,	*wit* (Fri.)

(It is bad.)

Shall we soon hear 'Wet the 'ook with a wetstone' for 'Whet the hook with a whetstone'?

Some Englishmen would say, 'The 'ammer is on the hanvil'; and some have been known to say, ''enry 'it 'orace with the 'ollow of 'is 'and,' for 'Henry hit Horace with the hollow of his hand.'

English mark-timewords (participles) are of two kinds—one of an ongoing time-taking, as 'the *rising* sun'; and another of the ended time-taking, as 'the *risen* sun'; and they are of a few sundry shapes, some ending with *-en, -n*, as *broken*, and others ending with *-ed, -d*; and some without an ending, as *cut*.

1. In *-en*, those which are of one breath-sound, and moulded so that the bygone time-shape takes the sound (7) *o*[2]:—

Bore, borne.

Broke, broken.

Chose, chosen.

Clove, cloven.

Drove, driven.

Froze, frozen.

Rode, ridden.

Rose, risen.

Shore, shorn.

Smote, smitten.

Spoke, spoken.

Stole, stolen.

Strode, stridden.

Strove, striven.

Swore, sworn.

Tore, torn.

Throve, thriven.

Trode, trodden.

Wore, worn.

2. Some one-sounded and moulded time-words, of the sound (8) in the shape for bygone time, take -*en*, -*n*; as,

Draw, drew, drawn.

Grow, grew, grown.

Know, knew, known.

Throw, threw, thrown.

Flow, flew, flown.

Slay, slew, slain.

Unmoulded time-words take -*ed*, but a few of them take -*ed* or -*en*; as,

Grave, graved, graved, graven.

These following, as is shown by the Saxon, ought to take -*ed* rather than -*en*:—

- Hew.
- Rive.
- Show.

Shape, shave, and *swell* were in Saxon moulded, and thence took -*en*.

There is a set of time-words which were weak, but are now endingless in their mark-word shape. They ended with a roof-penning -*t* or -*d*, and the roof-penning of the ending -*ed* ran at last into the roof-penning of the stems in the way shown on p. 22, and their mark-word shapes are the same as those for bygone time.

- Cast.
- Cost.
- Cut.
- Hit.
- Let.
- Put.
- Rid.
- Set.
- Shoot.
- Shut.
- Split.
- Spread.
- Shed.

Shortened Shapes (p. 23).

- Bred.
- Crept.
- Dealt.
- Fed.
- Fled.
- Left.
- Lost.
- Slept.
- Sped.
- Spilt.
- Swept.
- Wept.

One-sounded root time-words are mostly endingless in their mark-word shape:—

Sin	san	*sun*
g,	g,	g.

WORDS OF SPEECH-CRAFT, AND OTHERS, ENGLISHED.

WITH SOME NOTES.

Ablative (fromness case). The case of the source of the time-taking.
Abnormal. Unshapely, queer of shape, odd.
Abrade. To forfray, forfret. For *for-* see <u>For-</u> hereafter.
Absist. Forbear.
Absorb. Forsoak.
Absolute. *Checkless*, freed or loosened from checks.
Absolve. To forfree-en, forloosen.
Abstract (in speech-craft). Unmatterly, not of matterly form.
Accelerate. To onquicken, quicken.
Accent. Word-strain, a strain of the voice, higher or lower, on a breath-sound.
Accessary. A bykeeper, deedmate.
Accidence. The forshapenings of words for case, tale, time, mood, or person.

Accusative (case). End-case, the case of a thing which is the end or aim of a time-taking.
Acephalous. Headless.
Acoustics. Sound-lore, hearing-lore.
Active. Sprack (Wessex), doingsome, doughty.
Active (time-taking). One that can reach from the time-taker to another thing; as, 'to strike.' John can strike another thing.
Acute. Sharp or high in sound.
Adjective. Thing-markword, mark-word.
Adulation. Flaundering, glavering.
Adverb. An under-markword.
Adversative. Thwartsome.
Aerology. Air-lore.
Aeronaut. Airfarer.
Affirmation. Foraying, or a *foryeaing*, not a *fornaying*; as, 'Yes, he is.'
Agglutinate. To upcleam, to cleam up.
Aggregate. The main, whole.
Allative (case). A name given by some writers to that of a thing at which the time-taking is aimed (the aim case).

Alienate. To unfrienden.

Allegory. A forlikening.

Alliteration. Mate-pennings (*i.e.* Breath-pennings).

Alone. *All-án*, all-one:—'Nen manniska buta God *al ena.*γράψον'—W. Friesic. 'No man, but God all-one (alone.)'

Altercation. A brangle, brangling, brawling.

Ambiguous. Twy-sided, twy-meaning:—'Alfred was struck as he was walking with a stout stick.' *Struck* or *walking* with a stick? (twy-sided.) 'Those shoes were made before the man that made them.' *Before* in time, or *before* not behind?

Amicable. Friendly:—'We have lived in amicable relations' (friendly, in friendliness).

Amphibious. Twy-breath'd, twy-aired: by lungs and gills.

Amphibology. A twy-casting, a wording of two meanings.

Amphimacrum. Long sidelings, long end-sounds. A foot (in verse) of one short sound between two long ones, or of a low sound between two high ones; as, Tó and fró.

Amputate. Forcarve.

Anachronism. A mistiming.

Anagram. A letter-shuffling; as, out of 'name' to
1234
make 'mane,' or of 'march' to make 'charm.'
3214

Analysis. A forloosening or unmaking of a word or wording, or any thing, into its sundry clear pieces.

Anastrophe. A word-shifting; as, 'Fasten it *up well*,' 'Fasten it *well up*.' 'He brought *back* the horse,' or 'He brought the horse *back*.' 'There is none to dispute *my right*,' or '*My right* there is none to dispute.'

Anastrophe affords a case Of the shifting of words from place to place.

Ancestor. Fore-elder, kin-elder.

Animate. To quicken.

Annals. Year-bookings.

Annihilate. To fornaughten.

Anniversary. Year-day.

Annuity. Year-dole.

Antanaclasis. Twy-hitting on a word:—'If *shape* that was which had no *shape*.' 'It is the best *art* that conceals *art*.'

By antanaclasis is heard Aloud once more a former word.

Anodyne. Pain-dunting, pain-dilling. (*Dill*, *-n*, to dunt, to soothe.)

Anomalous. Odd-shaped, oddly shapen.

Antepenultimate (breath-sound). Last but two.

Anticipate. To foreween, foretake.

Antique. Ancient, *fore*old, *ere*old. *Old* for things in being, *fore*old or *ere*old for things forgone.

Antithesis. An atsetting.

Antonomasia. Name-shunning, the marking of a man by other words than his name; as, 'The honourable member for A.,' instead of 'Mr. B.'

Aphæresis. Foredocking of a word; as, *pothecary* for *apothecary*, *nob* for *knob*.

Aphorisms. Thought-cullings.

Apocope. End-lopping; as *mortal* for *mortalis*, *send* for *send-an*.

Apodosis. The hank time-taking to a hinge one (*protasis*):—'If ye ask (hinge), ye shall receive (hank).'

Aposiopésis. A tongue-checking; as, 'Do you think——but I reck not what you think.'

Apostrophe. An offturning.

Appellative (name). A call-name.

Appendix. Hank, hank-matter.

Apposition. A twy-naming, a putting of two names for one thing; as, 'The dog Toby.'

Aptote. Casemarkless.

Aqueduct. Waterlode.

Arbitrator. Daysman (Job ix. 33).

Armistice. A weapon-staying, weapon-stay, war-pause.

Articulation. Breath-penning.

Aspirate. A breathing, hard breathing.

Assimilate. To make of the same *sam* (form of matter) or *lic* (bodily form of a thing). To assimilate food, to forselfen it, to make it into a man's self.

Asylum has with us widely shifted its first meaning. An *asylon* was a sanctuary where a man was *asylos*, not to be pulled away (from *a*, *sylao*) by a foe. Now it often means a place whence a man cannot get away.

Asyndeton. Linklessness. The putting of words without link-words; as, 'Faith, hope, charity,' for 'Faith *and* hope *and* charity.'

Asyndeton puts side by side Strong words, by ne'er a linkword tied.

Atmosphere. Welkin-air.

Attraction. A *fordrawing*, a drawing of a word out of its true case or tale by another word to which it is nearer than to the one which it should match; as,

'Neither of the men *are* (for *is*) come.' Where the time-word would most likely have been drawn into the somely shape by its nearness to men.

Attraction may be *misdrawing*.

Augment. An eking, eking on or out.

Auxiliary. Outeking or helping.

Be- (a fore-eking, meaning *by*, *to*, *about*). *Bebutton* a coat, to put buttons to it; *becloke* school-children, give them clokes; *becloud*, obnubilate; *beflood*, inundate; *behem*, bebound or circumscribe; *bereek*, fumigate.

Belligerent. War-waging.

Bibulous. Soaksome.

Bicornous. Twy-horned.

Bidental. Two-teeth, two-teethed.

Bilateral. Two-sided:—'These articles would be considered a public *bilateral* contract, and would form the subject of an agreement with the Powers having Catholic subjects.' *Bilateral* contract is put for *bipartite*, a contract by or between two sides, or of men of two sides; but it would seem that the Romans did not call the two sides in a contract or cause *latera*, but *partes*—'Parte utrâque auditâ.'—*Plin. Jun.*

Latera are the sides of a body or space.

Binocular. Two-sighted.

Bipennated (as an axe). Twy-bladed.

Botany. Wortlore.

Cardinal (numbers). Tale-numbers; as, one, two, three.

Catachresis. A misuse (of a word); as, an *iron milestone*; a *parricide* for one who has killed his mother; *dilapidated* for a ragged coat.

Chemistry. Matter-lore, the science of matter.

Chronology. Time-lore.

Cinereous. Ash-grey.

Circular (a trade-circular). A touting-sheet or -bill.

Circumference. Rim, rimreach.

Circumflex. A roundwinding, a winding of the voice up and down again.

Clause. A word-cluster in a thought-wording.

Cognate. Kin, akin. *Cognate* breath-pennings; as, **T**, **D**, both on the roof.

Collective (name). That of a cluster or a many or a body of single things; as, a club, a herd.

Colon. Gr. *kōlon*, a limb or member. A mark for a limb, or marked share of a thought-bewording.

Colophon. Book-end.

Comma. Gr. *komma*, a cut or share. A mark for the offcutting of small shares of a discourse.

Complement. An *upfilling* or *outfilling* in words.

Compound. Clustered or a cluster, a clustered word, as *horseman*, or a thought-wording of two or more smaller ones.

Concord. A matching.
Concrete. Matterly.
Conditional (mood). Hinge-mood (p. 34).
Conjugation (of a time-word). The forfitting of it, the fortrimming of it.
Conjunction. A link-word.
Conjunctive. Linked, byholding.
Consonant. A letter for any breath-penning.
Construction. A word-setting, speech-trimming (see p. 36).
Contraction. An updrawing:—*I'll* for I will, *sinn'd* for sinnèd.
Co-ordinate. Rank-mate, row-mate.
Copula. A link or bond.
Correlative (words). Mate-words.
Crasis. Sound-blending, sound-welding.

Dactyl. Gr. *daktylos*. A foot (in verse) of one long and two short sounds, or of one high and two low sounds, as *cheerily*.

Dative. Giving.

Deciduous (plant). Fallsome. (Does it mean that only the leaves fall, or that the whole stem falls?) An elm is summer-green or leaved, and winter-sear. Holly is ever-green or winter-leaved. Parsley or the nettle is summer-stemm'd and winter-fallsome.

Decimate. To tithe:—'Breech-loading rifles would so decimate columns.' *Decimate* (*decimo*, from *decem*, ten, in Latin) was to take for death every tenth man of a body that had behaved very badly. The word *decimate* is now used very loosely, as meaning to cut up.

Defective. Wanting of something of its kind.

Defective (verb). Wanting of some time-shapes, as *quoth, must, go*. The foretime shape of *go* (*gang*) would be, as that of an unmoulded time-word, *goed*; and *goed*, a worn shape of the older '*gaode*,' is found in northern folk-speech, with *yowed* (Saxon *eode*.) *Gang* makes *ganged*.

Deficiency. Underodds. Excess, overodds.

Define. L. *de*, off; *finio*, to mark. To offmark.

Demagogue. Folk-leader, folk's-ringleader, folk's-reder.

Democracy. Folkdom.

Dental. L. *dentes*, teeth. A dental breath-penning is one more or less on the teeth; as, *eth, ef*.

Dependency. Beholdingness:—'As if one member would continue his wellbeing without *beholdingness* to the rest.'—*Carew*.

Depilatory. Hairbane.

Depletion. Unfullening.
Depopulate. Unfolk, forwaste.
Deport. Behave.
Deposit (of money). Earnest, pledge, bewaring.
Deprave. Forshrew, forwarp.
Depraved. Wicked.

Desecrate. Unhallow.
Desolate. Forloned.
Deter. Forfray.
Deteriorate. Worsen.
Develop. Unfold, unroll.
Diacritical. Offmarking, offskilling, sunder-clearing.
Diæresis. An outsundering or outopening, or foropening or forsundering, of a sound into two; as, L. *sylva*, *syl-wa*, into *syl-u-a*.
Diæresis splits sounds in two, As if for *true* you said *tri-u*.
Diagram. A draught, offdrawing.
Dialect. A sunder-speech, a folk-speech, a fortongueing.
Diaphanous. Thoroughshining, thoroughshowing.
Dictionary. A word-book.
Didactic. Teaching, teachsome.
Disease. The Saxon-English had about fifty pure Teutonic names of diseases, to the main of which we now give Latin names. They were ranked under some few head-words.

Cwealm (*qualm*) meant mostly a deadly or many-killing epidemic, as the plague or cholera, which they would call a *mancwealm* (*manqualm*). Of this word we have left only *qualm* with *qualmish*.

Adl (our *addle*) was another main word for disease, as an unsoundness. From this word we have *addle-headed* and an *addled* egg.

Coða, *code*, was another main word for a disease. Hence (Dorset) a *cothed* sheep.

Weorc, *werc* (our *wark*), was a disease of pain or achingness, as the gout or colic.

Seoc, *syc*, meant any *sickness* in which a man sinks down on his bed or is off his legs.

Bræc or *breach* was also given for some ailings.

To these words were set others of the parts of the body which they took, or of some other marks.

Stic-adl, stitch.
Sid-adl (side-addle), pleurisy.

Lengten-adl, lent-adl, typhus.
Hip-werc (hip-wark), sciatica.
Hrop-werc (bowel-wark, belly-wark (York)), colic.
Fylle seoc, falling sickness.
Lifer seoc, liver sickness.
Lifer-adl (Aelfric), liver-addle.
Milte-seoc (Aelfric), milt-sickness.
Lenden-wyrc (Aelfric), loin-wark.
Mete-afluing (Aelfric), atrophy.
Wylde-fyr (wildfire) (Aelfric), erysipelas.

Dissipate. Forscatter.

Distribution (of prizes). Outdealing, fordealing, outgiving:—'Uetdieling fen da pryzen.'—*Frs.* (outdealing of the prizes.)

-dom (an ending). It is our word *doom*, from *deem*, and means a state or outreach of free judgment or power; as, *kingdom, freedom*.

-dom. 'The scoundreldom and the rascality of a great city.' *Scoundrelhood.* Dom (from *deman*, to judge or rule) would be good for kingdom, popedom, sheriffdom, or mayordom. Scoundreldom would mean the might of scoundrels as ruling or judging.

Domicile. Abode, wonestead.

Ecthlipsis. An outcasting or outstriking, as of a sound; as, 'Sing *th' Almighty's* praise' for '*the Almighty's*,' or '*I'll go*' for '*I will* go.'

Ecthlipsis happens where one leaves Out sounds, or for *the eaves* says *th' eaves*.

Elative (case). The fromward case; as, 'He came from the house.'

Electricity. Matter-quickness; not speed, but liveliness. The word electricity means, as a word, only amberishness.

Ellipsis. An outleaving, as of a word understood; as, 'I went to St. Paul's' (church).

Ellipsis is of any word Well understood, but yet not heard.

-el (an ending). It means smallness or slightness:—*Dazzle*, to daze; *fraze*, frizzle; *nose*, nozzle (p. 18).

Embrasure. Gun-gap, cannon-gap.

Emphasis. Speech-loudening, speech-strain.

Emporium. Warestore.

Enallage. Case-shifting, an onchanging, as of a word or case into or for another; as, 'He was father to (or of) the fatherless.' 'The child took the toy in (or with) her hand.'

Enallagē takes word or case, To put it in another's place.

-en-ing (an ending). It means a becoming such; as, *blacken*, to make or become black; *blackening*, the becoming black.

The ending *-en-ing* differs from *-ness*, *-en-es*, as in *blackness*, which means the having become such.

Enthesis. An insetting.

Epenthesis. An inputting or inthrusting or infoisting of a sound or clipping into a word.

Epenthesis, for little good, Infoisteth aught, as *l* in *could*.[3]

Epithet. A mark-word put to a thing; as, 'The *far-shooting* Apollo,' 'the *white-blossom'd* sloe.'

Equilibrium. Weight evenness.

Equivalent. Worth evenness.

-er-r (an ending). It means outeked in size or time:—*Chatter*, to chat much; *clamber*, to climb much; *wander*, to wind about (pp. 18, 59).

Esculent (plant). Meatwort.

Etymology. Word-building, word-making, word-shaping.

Euphemismus. A fair wording, or the putting of bad or unworthy things in a fairer light by words of less evil meanings; as, 'I did time' for 'I was in prison.' 'A government man' for 'a convict.'

By euphemismus men are glad To make a bad case seem less bad.

Euphony. Sound softness, sound sweetness.

Exalt. Forheighten:—'Sa hwa him selma *forheaget*' (whoever himself forheightens).—*Friesic* (Matt xxiii. 12).

Excrescence. Outgrowth.

Exegetical. Outclearening.

Exordium. Outsetting, outset.

Expansion. Outbroadening of wild or overwrought fullness readily becomes a bad kind of wordiness:—'Farmer Stubbs drank beer,' 'The votary of Demeter, who rejoiced in the name of Stubbs, indulged in potations of the cereal liquor'; or 'He received me with the most lively indications of amity' for 'He received me very kindly'; or for 'He owes ten thousand pounds,' 'He is in a state of indebtedness to the extent of ten thousand pounds'; 'He warned the hunters off his land,' 'He conveyed to the votaries of Diana a strong admonition that they would not be permitted to prosecute their sport within his domain.'

Faculty. Makingness.

Filiaceous. Threaden.

Flexible. Bendsome.

Fluctuate. Waver.

Foliate. Leafen.

For-. The fore-eking of forgive, forbear, is a most useful one. It is the Anglo-Saxon *for*, the German *ver*, and the Latin *per*, and means off or away.

For-go, per-eo, to go off or away.

Per-suadeo (L. *suadeo*, from *suavis*), to soften or sweeten off.

Foreshorten and *forego* should be *forshorten* and *forgo*.

Forceps. Tonglings, nipperlings.

Fore- (a fore-eking). *Foredoom*, predestinate; *fore-token*, portent, omen (p. 61).

Fossil. A forstonening.

Frangible. Breaksome.

Garrulity.[4] Wordiness, talksomeness.

Genealogy. Kin-lore, kinhood-lore.

Genitive (case). The offspring case (p. 30).

Genuflexion. Knee-bowing. Much has been said (in the law trials about posture in the administration of the Holy Communion) of genuflexion. A genuflexion is any *knee-bowing*, but all knee-bowing is not kneeling, which is *knee-grounding*.

Glossarist. A word-culler.

Glossary. Gr. *glossa*, tongue, speech. A word-list or word-list:—'Mei en *lyst* vin oade spreckworden' (with a list of old saws).—*Friesic.*

Grandiloquent. High-talking.

Gratuitous. Out of kindness. *Gratia* is good will, free kindness; and *gratuitus* is freely bestowed of *gratia*, without hire or reward. But a writer says that an attack of slander on a woman's purity 'was gratuitous,' or of *gratia* or good will, without hire or reward, as if *gratuitous* meant without grounds of malice.

Hendiadys. One-in-twice. A wording of one thing at twice, or as two things; as, 'I heard shouting and men' for 'shouting of men.' 'An arm and strength' for 'a strong arm.' A fortwaining.

Hendiadys will give you two Clear words where one alone would do.

Hexameter. Gr. *hex*, six; *metron*, measure, metre. A metre in Greek and Latin verse, lines of six feet.

-hood (an ending). It means a state of being, rank, or standing among other things:—*Childhood, manhood.*

Horizon. Sky-sill, sky-line.

Hybrid (word). L. *hybrida*, a mongrel.

Hydrophobia. Water-awe.

Hyperbaton. Gr. *hyper*, over; *baino*, to fare, go. An overfaring, an overshifting of words out of their more wonted or better ranking; as, 'What for,' for 'For what.' A 'speaking out' for an 'outspeaking.'

Hypallage. Word-shifting, case-shifting; as, 'We gave wind to our sails' for 'our sails to the wind.' 'The men were put to the sword,' though also 'the sword was put to the men.'

Hyperbolē. An overcasting or overshooting of the truth; as, 'The train went as swift as lightning.'

Hyperbolē, less right than wrong, O'ershoots the truth with words too strong.

Hyphen. A tie-stroke.

Hysterologia. A foreafter wording, forebehind or hinderforemost wording; as, 'He earned a florin, and worked all the day,' whereas he worked first, and so earned the florin.

Hysterologia's careless mind Puts last for first, and fore for hind.

Iambus. Gr. A foot (in verse) of one short or low and one long or high sound; as, *ago*, a low-high twin.

Idiom. Gr. *idioma*, from *idios*, one's own. A folk's-wording, a set form of words of any one speech or set of men; as, 'How do you do?' *Fr.*: 'Comment vous portez-vous?' (How do you bear yourself?) 'I have just dined.' *Fr.*: 'Je viens de dîner' (I come from to dine).

Imperative (mood). The bidding mood.

Impersonal (verb). A time-word without a thing-name; as, 'It lightens,' 'it thunders,' 'it freezes,' 'it thaws.' A *thingnameless* or a deederless time-word.

Impertinence may be meddlesomeness in what *non pertinet*, does not belong to one, or meddlesomeness in a deed or speech which *non pertinet*, does not *hold* by the matter under thought, *unbyholdingness*.

Impertinent. Meddlesome, unbyholding.

Inarticulate. Unbreathpenned.

Incandescent. White-hot, heat-whitened.

Inceptive (verbs). Belonging to ontaking or beginning. *Becomesome* time-words; as, L. *albesco*, to become white; English *whiten*, to become or make white. In Greek the ending of the becomesome words is *-iz* or *-z*. *Orphanízo*, to make or become elderless, or an orphan.

Indefinite. L. *in*, un; *finio*, to offmark, outmark. *Unoffmarked, unbounded*.

Indicative (mood). The surehood mood.

Infinitive (mood). L. *in*, un; *finitus*, bounded, marked. The unboundsome thing-free mood of a time-word free of anything; as, to love, to see.

Initial. Word-head.

Injury. *Injuria* is a moral wrong (summum jus summa injuria). Do we not wrest its meaning in such wording as 'The wind has done much *injury* to my house-roof' or '*injured* my flowers'? How can the behaviour of the wind be made out to be a moral wrong, even if it be a hurt?

Instrumentive, instrumental (case). The *tool-case* or *means-case*, that of the tool or means of a deed; as, 'He cut the wood with a knife.'

Interest (of money). Money-rent, loan-meed, loan-pay.

Interest. Care:—'I do not take any *interest* in him or it.' 'I do not becare him or it.' 'Wha kara unsis?' (what care to us) (Mœso-goth).—Matt. xxvii. 4.

What a word to be taken as a thing-name is *interest*, 'it is of odds'! The folk-speech, 'It is of no odds to me,' gives the meaning of 'meâ non interest.'

Intransitive. Not overgoing, as time-takings that do not reach forth to another thing; as, to *sleep*.

Inversion. L. *inverto*, to turn up. An end-shifting:—'Thee at morn, and Thee I praise at night,' for 'I praise Thee at morn, and Thee at night.' A shifting of the ends of a wording.

Irony. Gr. *eirōneia*, from *eiron*, a shammer. A good wording for a bad meaning, *mock-praise*; as, 'That was a *good* shot,' meaning a very *bad* one. 'He is a *nice* man,' meaning the reverse of *nice*. 'How *glorious* was the king of Israel to-day!' meaning how *inglorious*.

-ism. The stump *-ism* of the Greek *-ismos* seems to be used very loosely. *-ismos* is from the ending *-izō* of ontaking or inceptive time-words, and where there is no time-word ending in *-izō* there is not, I should think, any thing-name in *-ismos*; as, *chloros*, green; *chlorizō*, to become green; *chlorismos*, a becoming green. So, if liberalism is a becoming *liberal*, conservatism is a becoming *conservat*, which might seem to mean *conservatus*, one conserved, rather than a conserver. Is chartism a becoming a *chart*? and what is Londonism, a becoming *London* or a *Londoning*? and, if so, what is a Londoning?

We have for *-ismos* some English endings, as *-ening*, in *blackening*; besides *-hood*, *-ship*, and *-ness*, and many others of sundry kinds.

For *-ism*, taken in names bestowed with very slight praise, we may take *-ishness*; as, *Hebraism*, Hebrewishness; *Grecism*, Greekishness; *Latinism*, Latinishness; *Londonism*, Londonishness; *solœcism*, folkswording. (On 'Solœcism,' see Aul. Gell. v. 20.)

Iterative. Going over again and again. Iterative time-words, that mean to take many shorter times in time-takings of the same kind; as, to *chatter*, chat much; *clamber, wander*.

Labial (letter). L. *labium*, lip. A lip breath-penning.

Laxative. Loosensome.

Lecture. A lore-speech.

Lenis. L. *soft*. The soft breathing is an *unaspirate* one, such as *a* in *and*, not *ha* in *hand*.

Letter. L. *litera*; Sax. *bóc-staf*, a book-staff. It is bad that the same word *letter* should be used for a *letter* of the alphabet and an *epistle*, the old English word for which is a *brief*, as it is in German and West Friesic. It was also the name of the king's letter for gathering of help-money in the church; though now it is the name only of a barrister's letter of instruction.

Lingual. L. *lingua*, the tongue. Belonging to the tongue.

Literature. Book-lore.

Lithography. Stone-printing.

Locative (case). L. *locus*, stead, place. The stead or stow-case; as, 'In London,' 'At church.'

Logic. Redelore.

-m, -om, -um. A word-ending, a form of the Greek one *-ma*, as in *prag-ma*, from *prasso*; and of the Latin *-men*, as in *flu-men*, from *fluo*. Words so ended meant mostly the outcome of the time-word, and were at first thing-names; and so as time-words they were, as most of them yet are, weak ones. From roots ending, I believe, in *-ing* came[5]

Blow	Bloom.
Cling (*root*)	Clome (clay or clayen pottery), clam, climb.
Cring (*root*) (to bend)	Crome (a dung-pick with bent prongs).
Dunt, ding(*root*)	Dam, dim, dumb, damp (fire).
Go (with quick stirrings), —ging (*root*)	Game.
Glow	Gleam, gloom.
Grow	Groom (a growing or now full-grown youth?).
Hollow	Haulm, helm, helmet.
Harry	Harm.
Lose, lithe, (ling *r.*)	Limp, limb, lime, loam.
Shriek	Scream.
Sew	Seam.
Slack,—sling (*root*)	Slam (a slackness or looseness in matter or going; slam of a gate; a slack swing, as unguided by a hand).
Slack	Slime, slim.
Stiff or stout	Stem.
Stray or Stretch on	Stream.[6]
Tang, ting (reach on)	Team, time, and timer, timber (a very ontanging stick).
Thick	Thumb (the thick finger).

Machine. An old English word for a machine is *ginny* or *jinny* which seems to be a fellow-stem to *gin*, and to mean *to go*, not as in onfaring (locomotion), but as in the way of a machine.

Magnificent. High-deedy, high-doing.

Magniloquent. High-talking.

Mechanics. Matter-might.

Metalepsis. Gr. *metalambano*, to take over. A *use-shifting* of a word, a taking of a word over from its common to another meaning; as, 'Seven harvests ago' for 'seven summers or years.'

Metaphor. Gr. *metaphora*, from *metaphero* to carry over. A figure of speech, the overcarrying of a name from a thing to which it belongs to another to which it does not belong; as, 'The *Shepherd* of Israel' for 'the Lord.' 'The *father* of the people' for 'a good king.' '*Eos* Cymru' (the Welsh *nightingale*) for 'a fine Welsh songstress.' 'A man *burning* with anger.'

Metathesis. Gr. *meta*, with or against; *thesis*, a putting. A penning-shift, as that of putting each of two pennings in the stead of the other; as, wa*ps*, wa*sp*; ha*ps*; ha*sp*; though the first of the two shapes is the older in English.

Metathesis is where a word Shifts pennings, as in *crud* for *curd*.

Meteor. Welkin-fire.

Metonymy. Gr. *meta*, off; *onoma*, a name. An *offnaming*, *name-shifting*, a wording that puts for a thing-name the name of some belonging—whether cause or effect or aught else—of the thing; as, 'He reads *Horace*' for '*his works*.' 'He lives by *the sweat of his brow*' for '*work*.' 'Land holden by the *Crown*' (*Queen*). 'The power of the *pen*' for '*writers*.'

Miosis. Gr. *meiōsis*, a forlessening. A wording by which a thing is lessened off; as, 'Will you give me a *crumb* of bread and a *drop* of drink?'

Miōsis, a lessening, Makes of a great a smaller thing.

Monitor. A warner. Ware-en-er, who makes ware.

Monosyllable. A breath-sound.

Multiloquous. Wordy, talksome.

Negative (word). L. *nego*, to deny. Fornaysome.

Nomenclature. Benaming, name-shapening.

Nominative. L. *nomen*, a, name. The name-case, speech-case.

Noun. L. *nomen*, a name; Fr. *nom*. A thing-name, thing-word, name-word.

Objective. Objective case. A name commonly given to the time-giving thing when it is not the speech-case.

Onomatopœia. A mocking name. The making of words from sounds; as, to *hiss*, a *peewit* or *cuckoo* from the sound it makes.

Optative (mood). The wish mood; as, 'Oh! that I had wings.' 'May you be happy.'

Out- (a fore-eking). *Outban*, exile; *outfaring*, peregrination, exodus; *outhue*, *outliken*, depict or draw.

Over- (a fore-eking). *Overbold*, audacious; *overhang*, impend; *overweigh*, preponderate.

-p, -b, -f (endings). They mean small in kind or short in time:—Poke, *pop*, poke quickly; *dip*, a small dive; *slip*, a small slide; *rip*, to rive quickly.

Palindrome. Gr. *palin*, back; *dromos*, a running. A set of words which read the same backwards as forwards; as, 'Lewd did I live, evil I did dwel,' or 'Roma tibi subito motibus ibit amor.'

A palindrome's the same as read From head to tail, or tail to head.

Palpitate. Throb.

Panacea. Allheal.

Paradigm. Gr. *paradeigma*, an offshowing, outshowing, a plan. A table of word-shapes.

Paragogē. An outbringing or outlengthening of a word.

A paragogē will be found Where words are lengthened by a sound.

'Such a sweet pett as this Is neither far nor *neary*. Here we go up, up, up; Here we go down, down, *downy*. Here we go backwards and forwards, And here we go round, round, *roundy*.'

Old Song.

'In playhouses, full *six-o*, One knows not where to *fix-o*.'

Old Song.

Paragraph. An offwriting, a wording-share; such a share of a piece of writing as, if it were offwritten, would not want anything of a full meaning.

Paraphrase. New bewording; a turning of a piece of writing into other words, often more if not clearer than those of the writer. A paraphrase, while it is meant to clearen, may falsen the paraphrased matter. The following paraphrase from an old written sermon of (as I believe) an old Dorset divine, may be a good sample of new bewording:—

'God, I thank Thee, that I am not as other men are, extortioners, unjust, adulterers, or even as this Publican: I fast twice in the week, I give tithes of all that I possess.'

Expanded or paraphrased:—

'With great gratitude, O God (said the Pharisee), I contemplate my own superior attainments. How free is my mind from a variety of black offences which invade the consciences of others! Extortion, injustice, and adultery are crimes (said he, striking his breast) which have no harbour here. Who can lay to my charge the neglect of any religious duty? Are not my tithes paid with cheerfulness, and my fasts observed with sanctity?'

'And the Publican, standing afar off, would not lift up so much as his eyes unto heaven, but smote upon his breast, saying, God be merciful to me a sinner.'

'The Publican, on the other hand, with every mark of the deepest contrition, stood abashed in a corner of the temple. Conscious of his own demerits, he was afraid to raise his eyes to that Being who sees the least degree of impurity with offence. After many ineffectual struggles to form the sighing of a contrite heart into the language of prayer, his efforts ended in this one exclamation, God be merciful to me a sinner.'

Parenthesis. An inwedging of a sentence within another:—'Thou sayest—but they are but vain words—I have strength for the war.'

Parody. A song-mocking.

Paronomasia. A kind of play on words of more or less like sound, though of sundry meaning; as, 'Though *last* not *least*.' 'Non amissi sed præmissi' (said of friends deceased), 'Not forgone but foregone.'

Paronomasia is found In pairs of words of some like sound.

Participle. A thing-marking shape of the time-word.

Particle. A wordling, a small shapefast word.

Patronymic. Gr. *pater*, father, and *onoma*, name. A surname or sirename of a man taken from the forename of his father; as, John Richardson, Dafydd Ap-hoel, Patrick Mac-Duff, Jeroboam Ben-Nebat.

Pedigree. Kin-stem, forekin-stem.

Penultimate. Last but one.

Perambulator (the child's carriage). Push-wainling.

Perfect. Fordone, forended, full-ended.

Period, in rhetoric (redecraft) and speechcraft, is so called, as a speech-ring or speech-round, a full round of thought-wording, in which the speech-meaning is kept uphanging and more or less unclear, till the last word or word-cluster by which it is clearly fulfilled; as, '(1) That among the sundry changes of the world (2), (3) our hearts may surely there be fixed (4): (5) where true joys are to be found (6).' The whole thought-wording is a period or speech-round. From (1) to (4) is a limb (called in Greek a *kōlon*) and has a meaning, though not a full one beyond which the mind awaits nothing more. The word-cluster from (1) to (2) yields no full meaning, and is called in Greek a *komma* (*kopma*), a cutting or shareling. Thence we see the source of the names and uses of the stops—the *period* (.), *colon* (:), *comma* (,). The *period* marked the end of the period; the *colon* that of the kolon; and the *comma* that of a comma, or cutting of a colon.

The word seems to be often misused. A *period* (Gr. *periodos*) of time or wording is rightly a running of it round again to its like beginning; as, a week—from Sunday round to Sunday; or a year—from January to January.

A straight stretch of time or words is not truly a period; as, a man's life from birth to manhood is not a ring-gate, beginning anew at childhood.

Periphrasis. Gr. *peri*, round; *phrasis*, a speaking. A roundabout speaking of a thing instead of an outright naming of it, a *name-hinting*; as, 'The gentleman at the head of Her Majesty's Government' for Lord B.

Personal (time-word); not an impersonal one; as, 'It rains.' 'It snows;' but one with a named time-taker, as 'John rides.'

Perverse. Wayward, froward.

Pervious. Throughletting.

Petrify. To stonen, forstonen.

Philology. Speechlore.

Phonetic. Soundly.

Phonography, **phonotypy**. Sound-spelling. Surely a photograph should be a phototype. *Graphō* is to graze or grave along a body, but a photograph is given by a plumb downstriking of rays of light—a *typē* and not a *graphē*. With *graphē* and *typē* we may set a *glyphē* (from *glyphō*), an outsmoothing of a shape, as that of a figure from a block of stone. *Glyphō* is a fellow stem-word to *glykys*, smooth, soft, or sweet.

Phrase. Gr. *phrazo*, to speak, say. A word-cluster, a word-set, a cluster or set of byhanging words.

Pirate. Sea-robber, weeking, wyking, wicing (Gloss. 11 cent.). The *wicings* or *weekings* or *vicings* were so called as lurking about in the bays, *wicas*, *weeks*, *wykes*, or *wiches*.

Plagiary. A thought-pilferer.

Pleonasm. Gr. *pleonazo*, to fullen or overfullen. An overwording; as, 'A great [thing of a] boar' for 'a great boar.' 'What [ever in the world] are you doing?' 'Never [in all my whole life] have I seen the like.'

A pleonasm oft is heard To strengthen speech by word on word.

Plocē. Gr. *plokē*, a twining or folding. A twining or folding of a foregiven name, of one meaning the same name, in another; as, 'Then Edwin was Edwin (or himself) again.' Worthy of himself. 'Coal is now coal,' *i.e.* scarce and costly.

By plocē you inweave a name Once more with meaning not the same.

Plural (number). The somely (number).

Polyptoton. Gr. *poly*, many; *ptotos*, case. The inbringing of fellow stem-words or root-words in sundry cases or ways:—'He, friendless once, befriended friends.'

Posterity. Afterkin.

Postposition. A hinder case-word, a case-word put after the thing-name; as, in Hindustani, *panee-main*, water in; *panee-sae*, water from; *panee-ko*, water to. Showing the source of case-endings.

Potential (mood). L. *potentia*, might, power. Mayly.

Predicate. The wording of the time-taking; as, 'John *walked twenty miles*.'

Prefix. A fore-eking, a forewordling; as, *be-set*, *for-give*, *out-run*.

Preposition. A case-word.

Preterite. Bygone, past.

Programme. A foredraught.

Pronoun (personal). A name-token, a stead-word. Pronoun Adjective, mark-word.

Proper name. A one-head name.

Prosopopœia. Gr. *prosopon*, face, person; *poieo*, to make. The putting of an unmatterly or impersonal thing as a person.

Prosopopœia shows your mind Unlive things doing as mankind.

Protasis. The hinge time-taking.

Prototype. Foreshape, forepattern.

Punctuation. L. *punctuatio*, from *puncta*, points or stops. The skill of the putting of stops, or of the marking of voice-stoppings in speech. Bestopping. (See 'Period.')

Radicle. Rootling.

Reciprocal (verb). L. *re*, back, fro; *ci*, to this way. To and fro verbs; as, 'They helped each other.'

Rectify. Righten.

Reflective. Back-turning, as a time-taking which comes back to the source of it; as, 'John cut or hit himself.'

Regimen. Government, overwielding of a thing by another.

Religion. Faith-law.

Religious. On the true meaning of *religiosus* see Aul. Gell. *Noct. Att.* iv. 9. He makes it mean withholden, backbound from some uses. *Religiosa delubra*, a shrine hallowed from common use; *religiosus dies*, a day withholden, as unlucky, from great undertakings. A religious man is one who is withholden by his faith and conscience from bad deeds.

Restrain. Inhold, forhold.

Result. Outcome, outworking, backspring. *Result* (from *resilio*, to spring back) is neither in sound nor meaning a better word than *outcome* or *outworking* or *froming, fromming*.

Rhetoric. Rede-speech.

Rhythm. Gr. *rhythmos*, number, as number of clippings or sounds in a line of verse. *Metre*, which meant at first tale of sounds rather than sound matching, which we call rime. *Rime* is not come to us from the Greek, but is the Saxon *rim* or *hrim*, tale or number.

'Manâ and misdædâ ungerím ealrâ' (a tale, beyond telling, of all wickednesses and misdeeds).—*Sermo Lupi ad Anglos.*

'Deer naet in da rime was' (who was not in the number).—*Old Friesic Law.*

Salubrious. Healthy, halesome.

Satellite. Henchman.

Scintillate. Sparkle.

Semi-detached houses. Twin-houses, a house-twin.

Sentence. L. *sentio*, to think, deem, feel. In speech-craft, an uttering of a thought, one thought-wording.

Septuple. Sevenfold.

-sh (an ending). It means quickness and smartness; as, *clang*, clash; *crack*, crash; *fly*, flash; *go*, gush; *hack*, hash. In markwords it means somewhat such;—*blackish, boyish.*

-ship (an ending). It means a shape or form of being:—*Friendship, mateship.*

Solœcisms. Gr. *soloikismos*, from the bad Greek of the *Soloikoi* in *Cilicia*. A miswording, barbarism, or, as an old Saxon gives it, 'a miscweðen word,' or a misquothing, a misqueathing.

We in a solœcismus find Miswording of a loreless mind.

Solstice. Sunsted. A.S. Sunanstede.

-some. The ending *-some* in such words as *aimsome, matchsome, yieldsome* seems, as we look to its true first meaning, to be a fitting one. A *sam* or *som* (some) meant at first a body of mingled matter or things. In its stronger meaning lumps of suet melted up into a soft body would be a *sam* or *som*; and potatoes boiled and mashed up would be a *sam*; and dough, if not flour itself, is a *sam* or *som*.

In the wider meaning of the word an upgathering of things, and even men, into a body or set is a *sam* or *som*. Thence we have our word *same* as well as the ending *-some* and the markword *some*:—'*Some* in rags, and *some* in jags, and *some* in silken gowns' (a *set* or body in rags, a *set* or body in jags, &c.).

Aimsome, yieldsome would mean of the *aim* or *yield* or *aiming* or *yielding* set or body.

Sam or *som* gives our words *same* and *so*. 'The *same* man' means the very man in *sam* or body or being. 'Are they Hebrews? *so* (same) am I.' Of that *sam* (am I). The Latin *se* is most likely a word of the same root:—'Lucius *se* amat' (Lucius loves *same* or his *sam*); and this is the meaning of our word *self*.

The Latin *similis* would mean of the *sam* or *same* kind; and 'to *summon* (*samen*) men' is to call them up into a *sam*, 'Suma êlanda thêr im likte' (some islands that pleased him).—*Oera Linda Book*.

Sophist. Wordwise.

Sophistry. Rede-guile, rede-cunning.

Spell. Sax. *spellian*, to tell, utter forth a word or a set of words.

Spell. A message or bewording, as in *Godspel* (Gospel), 'the good message.'

-st (an ending). It strengthens the meaning, as it does in *blackest*; blow, *blast*; brow, *breast*.

Stereography. Bulk-drawing.

Stereometry. Bulk-meting.

Stereotype. Block-type.

Subject. The speech-thing or thing under speech.

Subjunctive (mood). The hinge-mood; as, 'If ye ask, ye shall receive.'

Suffix. A wordling put on at the end of a word; as, man-*hood*, good-*ness*, kind-*ly*. End-eking, an on-eking, a word-ending.

Superlative. The highest pitch.

Supposititious. Underfoisted, undersmuggled.

Syllepsis. Gr. *syn*, up, together; *lēpsis*, a taking. An uptaking, upmating, comprehension, as of a second or third person with a first; as, 'I (1) and my brother (3) (we) learn Latin.'.
Syllepsis takes I, you, and he As first persons, and all called we.

Synalœpha. Gr. *syn*, up; *aleipho*, to smear. Sound-welding. The welding up of two sounds into one, or the end of one word into the head of the following. In Latin verse—'Conticuere omnes,' 'conticuer͡omnes,' 'conticuere‿omnes'—uttering the *e* and *om* in the time of one syllable. So in Italian—'In prato‿in foresta,' 'Sia l'alba‿o la sera,' 'Se dorme‿il pastor'—the *o i*, and *a o*, and *e i* are uttered as one syllable. In English—'Before the‿Almighty's throne.'
By synalœpha breath-sounds run A couple to the time of one.

Syncope. The cutting of a penning from within a word; as, 'He ha-s' for 'he haves,' 'Gospel' for 'Godspel.' The outcutting is truly an *outwearing* of the clipping.
A clipping's lost by syncope, As *subtle's* sounded minus *b*.

Synecdoche. Gr. *syn*, up; *ek*, out; *dochē*, a taking. An outtaking or outculling, as of a share of a thing for the whole, or the matter for the thing; as, 'a hundred heads' for 'a hundred men'; 'twenty hands' for 'twenty workmen'; 'a cricketer's willow' for his 'bat.'

Synonym. Gr. *syn*, together; *onyma* a name. Synonyms are words or names of the same meaning, twin-words; as, *rabbit* and *coney*, *volume* and *tome*, *yearly* and *annual*, *letter* and *epistle*. Twains of words are, however, less often synonyms than they are so called.

Syntax. Speech-trimming. A *trim* is a fully right or good state of a thing, the state in which it ought to be; and 'to trim' a thing is to put it in trim, or fully as it ought to be. 'To *trim* a boat,' to set it as it ought to be—upright, not heeling. 'To *trim* a bonnet or dress,' to put it fully as it ought to be. And so 'to *trim* a hedge': a man may think that, because much of the trimming of a hedge is done by cutting, a trimming is therefore a cutting. 'I am out of *trim*'; 'to *trim*,' as a man in politics, albeit it may not be to set himself morally as he ought to be, is to set himself as he thinks that he ought to be for the nonce.

Tautology. Word-sameness, a saying over again of the same thing or words.
Technical. Craftly.
Telegram. Wire-spell. (See Spell.)
Telegraph (the electric). Spell-wire.
Telescope. Spyglass.
Tense. Time.
Termination. A word-ending.
Tmesis. A word-cutting or splitting or outsundering; as, 'The child has *overthrown* the flower-pot.' By word-cutting or outsundering—'The child has *thrown* the flower-pot *over*.'

By tmesis you may oft outshare A word's two word-stems here and there.

Transitive is overfaresome; *intransitive*, unoverfaresome.

Triphthong. Gr. *tri*, three; *phthongos*, sound. A threefold sound.

Uncial. L. *literæ unciales*, text letters. Capital letters.

Under. *Undersea*, submarine; *underspan*, subtend; *underslinking*, subterfuge.

Up-. *Upclashing*, collision; *upthrong*, congregate.

Upmating. The upmating of the persons, called in Greek *syllepsis*, touches the use of the personal pronouns. A second or third person upmated with the first is reckoned as first, and a third upmated with the second is reckoned as second; as,

'That boat belongs to my brother (3) and me (1). *We* (1) bought it.'

'That is known only to you (2) and me (1). *We* know it.'

'I saw you (2) and your brother (3). *You* (2) were there.'

But persons are upmated as well from kindliness or civility as from the calls of speech-craft. Thus a speaker will often upmate himself with a hearer or another, as a mother may upmate herself with her child by *we*, instead of *thou* or *you*; as,

Here *we* go up, up, up; Here *we* go down, down, downy; Here *we* go backward and forward; And here *we* go round, round, roundy—

though the going is only that of the child.

A young man may say to a girl friend, 'How proud *we* are,' meaning '*you* are'; or a man may say of others who might not be very brisk at work, '*We* are not very strong to-day'; or a footman may upmate himself with the heads of the house with such wording as '*We* do not treat our guests so unhandsomely.'

Vocabulary. L. *vocabulum*, a word. A word-list, word-book, word-store.

Vocative (case). L. *voco*, to call. The call-case.

-y, -ig (an ending). It means eked with something:—*Snowy*, with snow; *dirty*, with dirt.

Zeugma. Gr., a yoking. A yoking of two things as to one time-word which would fit only one of them, another being outleft; as, 'The house which my own money, and not which my father bequeathed,' supply *bought* after 'money.'

The Power of the Word-endings.

Some of the small word-endings end themselves with a dead breath-penning, and others with a half-penning. The dead pennings seem to betoken, mostly, an ending, or shortening, or lessening, in time or shape; while the half-pennings do not seem to bound, or shorten, or lessen, the meaning of their body-words.

Dead Pennings.

-ock. Hill-ock.

-ed. I walk-ed (the time-taking ended).

-ig, now **-y**. Wind-ig, wind-y (an eking of wind).

-op, -p; -ob, -b. Flap, flip, a quick flying; heap, hop, hip, small highenings, or humps; pop out, to poke out quickly; clap the hands, to close them quickly; stub, a small stump; wallop, to wallow or well (roll) lightly, and so as water from a spring, or in boiling. We may think that we have two very fine words in *envelope* and *develope*, whereas they seem to be nothing better than the Teutonic *inwallop* and *unwallop*, to roll in and unroll. With *wallow* set the Latin *volvo* (walwo), to roll.

-t, -et. Forlessens.

Poke,	pocket.
Ball,	bullet.
Sock,	socket.

Half-Pennings.

do not so strongly, if at all, betoken endingness, or shortness, or smallness.

-m. A *stem* is of any length, but *stump* is short.

-en, -n. *Golden*, eked wholly in gold; *blacken*, to eke on freely in blackness.

-ing, as in *walking*, does not betoken any ending or shortening of a time-taking.

-er, -r, betokens eking out much in shape or time, as:—

Chat,	chatter.
Pat,	patter.
Clate,	clatter.

It so happens that while we have a dead penning, *-ed*, for the ended time-taking, as, 'he walked,' we have a half-penning for the ongoing time-taking, as, 'he walketh.' It is true that *-en*, a half-penning, is put for *-ed*, as an ending of some mark-time words, as *brok-en*, and that *-el*, *-l*, a half-penning, may seem to mean either much or small, as *prate*, *prattle* (prat-el). Time-words with these endings in full length are weak.

- Bloss-om-ed,
- Black-en-ed,
- Wall-op-ed,
- Chat-er-ed,
- Flitt-er-ed,

- Pock-et-ed,
- Prat-el-ed
- (prattled).

s strengthens the meaning of some root-heads, as:—

Melt, smelt.

Nip, snip.

Plunge, splunge.

Queeze, squeeze.

So, as an ending of the somely thing-name, it stretches its meaning from that of one to some ones, as *a hand, hands*—hands being more than a hand.

In the word-ending -st of *black-est*, the half-penning *s* freely forstrengthens *black*, and the dead-penning *t* seems to check its force, so that *blackest* means *black* strengthened, though not unboundedly so, but blackest of all the things taken with it.

-st has, I suppose, this meaning also as an ending of thing-names or time-words, as 'to *boast*,' the meaning of which is betokened by some other tongues to be to *bow* out much the breast or fore-body, the token of pride and boasting, as it is so often shown to our sight.

Bogan, to bow (Anglo-Saxon and Friesic), means 'to boast.'

Friesic—'Thi mâgy *bogade* uppa sinra snôdhed.' (The mâgy boasted (bowed) on his cunning.)—*Oera Linda Book.*

'Hia *bogath* ìmmer over geda êwa.' (They boast (bow) ever over good laws.)—*Oera Linda Book.*

The old British bard, Llywarch Hên, had in mind the same token of pride:—

—gnawd dyn Bronrain balch

(It is common for a proud (or boasting) man to be bow- or bulge-breasted); and in the Holderness (Yorkshire) folkspeech they say 'as *bug* (proud) as a dog wi' two tails,' and yet, to show that *bug* means a bow or bowedness, they say 'as *bug* as a cheese.'

The Goodness of a Speech.

The goodness of a speech should be sought in its clearness to the hearing and mind, clearness of its breath-sounds, and clearness of meaning in its words; in its fulness of words for all the things and time-takings which come, with all their sundrinesses, under the minds of men of the speech, in their common life; in sound-sweetness to the ear, and glibness to the tongue. As to fulness, the speech of men who know thoroughly the making of its words may be fullened from its own roots and stems, quite as far as has been fullened Greek or German, so that they would seldom feel a stronger want of a foreign word than was felt by those men who, having the words *rail* and *way*, made the word *railway* instead of calling it *chemin de fer*, or, going to the Latin, *via ferrea*, or than Englishmen felt with *steam* and *boat*, to go to the Greeks for the name of the *steamboat*, for which Greek had no name at all. The fulness of English has not risen at the rate of the inbringing of words from other tongues, since many new words have only put out as many old ones, as:—

immediately, anon,

(no saving of time here),

ignite, kindle,

annual, yearly,

machine, jinny.

I have before me more than one hundred and fifty so taken English law-words which were brought into the English courts with the Norman French tongue; but English speech did not therefore become richer by so many words, because most of them thrust aside English ones. *Judge* took the stead of *dema*; *cause* of *sác*; *bail* of *borh*; and the lawyers said *arson* for *forburning*; *burglary*, for *housebreach*; and *carrucate*, for *ploughland*; and King Alfred gave to English minds the matter of Gregory's Pastoral with a greater share (nearly all) of pure English words, than most English scholars could now find for it.

On clearness, it is to be feared that, notwithstanding the English may be clear in breath-sounds to the ear, there is often a want of clearness to the mind from the many pairs of words which have worn into the same sound, such as:—

Bow, bow,

Doe, dough,

Lea, lee,

Pale, pail,

So, sew,

w,

and others; and from the use of Latin and Greek and other foreign words, which are used in other than their true first meanings, or the meanings of which the common folk do not understand.

Teleology is a word which I have just seen in a Dorset paper, as for the matter of a lately given lore-speech, 'the examination or the discussion of the purposes for which things are created.' Now, in English the word *end* means both a *forending*, or termination, and a purpose; but I do not think that *telos* (end) or *teleosis*, in Greek, means a purpose. *Prothesis* would most likely have been put for it by a Greek.

The Latinish and Greekish wording is a hindrance to the teaching of the homely poor, or at least the landfolk. It is not clear to them, and some of them say of a clergyman that his Latinised preaching is too high for them, and seldom seek the church.

Swan is a clue to the meaning of *swanling* but none of *cygnet*; and if a man knew that *kyknos* was the Greek for swan he might still be at a loss for the meaning of *-et*, which is not a Greek ending.

For sound-sweetness or glibness, we should shun, as far as we can, the meeting of hard dead breath-pennings of unlike kinds. We have in our true English too many of them, and some of them from the dropping of the *e* from the word-ending *-ed*, as in *slep't* and *pack'd* (lip and roof, and throat and roof pennings, and in both cases hard dead pennings); and then, as if we had not enough of them, we have brought in a host more of such ones from the Latin, as in *act, tract, inept, rapt*.

Now, *forbend* is a softer-sounded word than *deflect*, since *ct* (kt) are hard throat and root pennings, very unhandy together, and the *n* of *-nd* is a mild half-penning, and *d* is a mild dead penning. So *dapper* is better sounded than *adept*, since *p* is a single hard penning between two free breathings, and *pt* are a hard lip and a hard roof breathing, unfollowed by any softer breathing.

It was against such harshness of hard unlike breath-pennings that Celtic speech took its markworthy word-moulding.

As a token of the readiness of two kindred breath-pennings to run into one, we may give the words of the Liturgy, 'Make clean our hearts within us,' for which a clergyman will hardly, without a pause and a strong pushing of the breath, help saying 'Make lean our hearts within us.'

There came out in print some time ago a statement wonderful to me, that it had been found that the poor landfolk of one of our shires had only about two hundred words in their vocabulary, with a hint that Dorset rustics were not likely to be more fully worded. There can be shown to any writer two hundred thing-names, known to every man and woman of our own village, for things of the body and dress of a labourer, without any mark-words, or time-words, or others, and without leaving the man for his house, or garden, or the field, or his work.

Footnotes

[1] 'Enaid yr ymadrod yw'r ferf.'

[2] See Table of Sounds, p. 1.

[3] From *cuðe*.

[4] The Welsh shows the source of this word in *gair*, a word; *gair-ol*, wordy.

[5] The words of the latter row are not shapen, at once, from those of the first one. Such of the first as are not roots in *-ing* are fellow stems to the others. As, *stem* from the root *sting*, to be more or less stiff or steadfast: sting, a stang, a stake, a stick. Steg-me (Gr. stigma), stegm (stem). *Stem* is not from *stick*, but from the root.

[6] In Welsh *avon*, a river, is from a time-word meaning to go on.

'Mi *av* i'r *avon* vawr rhag llosgi.' (I will go into the great river ere I be burned.)

Welsh Song.

Printed in Great Britain
by Amazon